Laura's
SAFE HAVEN

DANIELLE M HAAS

Cover created by Deranged Doctor Designs.

A Danielle M Haas Publishing Book

Laura's Safe Haven - Safe Haven Women's Shelter

For all the women who've stood strong, survived hardships, and found a dream to follow

A NOTE TO THE READER

To my wonderful reader,

Thank you so much for choosing to read Laura's Safe Haven. Before you begin, I wanted to let you know this book contains a story about a strong woman who has survived her abusive ex. The book contains themes of domestic abuse, both from a romantic partner and family member.

If you or anyone you know finds yourself in an abusive situation and you need someone to talk to, please call the National Domestic Violence Hotline at 1-800-799-SAFE (1-800-799-7233).

1

The late May sun beat down on Laura Metcalf as she sprayed cleaner on the windows in the lodge of Crossroads Mountain Retreat. The panes acted like a magnifying glass, intensifying the heat and causing sweat to bead at her hairline.

But she couldn't be more content.

Staring out at the Smoky Mountains with her muscles straining from hard work, all she could think was how far she'd come in the last few months. She'd finally left her abusive boyfriend, moved into her own place, and was learning to stand on her own two feet.

She cradled her growing baby bump. Pregnancy wasn't something she'd anticipated, but the fierce desire to keep her child safe had pushed her into finally walking away from the man who'd caged her in for so long. Now, at six months pregnant, all she needed to do was figure out what her future looked like for her and her baby.

No pressure.

"Windows look great!"

Laura spun around and grinned at her friend and boss,

Brooke Mather.

Okay, so boss might be a bit of an overstatement. Brooke was the owner of Crossroads Mountain Retreat, a place of physical and emotional healing for veterans and law enforcement. Most of the staff were from the same world as the people they assisted.

Laura wasn't, but Brooke had made an exception with her. Giving her odd jobs whenever she could while she figured out the mess she'd made of her life. A gesture that wasn't at all surprising from a citizen of Pine Valley, Tennessee. Here, neighbors were family, always willing to go the extra mile.

Something Laura desperately needed while still trying to navigate her own complex family dynamics.

"Thanks," she said, wiping away the stream of spray as it dripped toward the floor. "I think I'm done with everything on your list for the day. If there's nothing else you need, I'll get going. I'm working a shift at the Chill N' Grill tonight."

Another neighbor, another job, another small paycheck to go toward her pile of unpaid bills.

Brooke brushed a wisp of brown hair behind her ear and took a step forward.

Laura struggled not to flinch. Brooke wasn't trying to invade her personal space. She wasn't here to reprimand or punish her. But years of dealing with an abuser—a lifetime really—made some habits hard to break.

"Before you go, I wanted to let you know I spoke with your brother today."

"Oh yeah? What about?" She swiped her palms on the thighs of her worn jeans.

"I talked to him about taking on the construction job for expanding the food pantry in town."

"I'm sure Matthew would love the job. His company is amazing." She might not know that for sure but didn't see why her brother's construction company wouldn't be a top contender for the work. He and his business partner were responsible for a lot of the growth in the community, as well as the surrounding areas.

"He said he planned to be out of town for a chunk of time. Then he directed me to your father, who's utilizing the Community Outreach Fund for the pantry's expansion, to discuss a bid. I'm hoping it works out."

She forced a tight smile at the mention of her father, the mayor of Pine Valley. He might not have left visible bruises throughout her childhood, but he'd left plenty of scars. Scars that ran so deep she doubted she'd ever be able to outrun them.

"I wonder where Matthew's going? He never mentioned anything."

Brooke shrugged. "He didn't say. Just that Cade would be the point person, and he hoped to talk to you about helping while he's away."

Her cheeks warmed at the mention of her brother's best friend. Being alone for hours on end with Cade Sulley might have been something she'd fantasized about as a teenager, but that was a lifetime ago. These days she couldn't even look Cade in the eyes, not that she saw much of him. "Me? I have no experience working for a construction company."

"Did you ever have experience at a bar or around a retreat prior to a few months ago?" Brooke's small smile told Laura she already knew the answer.

"No."

"Then there's no telling what other things are out there waiting for you to discover. All you have to do is try."

Laura sighed, allowing herself one quick second of self-pity. If only life was that easy—that things were really so simple. The reality was she had no work experience, no education beyond a high school diploma she'd barely earned, and a truckload of trauma to unpack. The only thing she could focus on was survival.

Brooke frowned. "Sorry. I didn't mean to simplify your situation. You've been through hell. You know everyone in this town is behind you, cheering for you."

"Thanks," she said, meaning it to her core. "Taking the first step is sometimes the hardest, but that doesn't mean it gets any easier. I just need to keep moving—pushing forward—grateful for where I am. The rest will fall into place."

She had to believe that was true. That at twenty-two she still had time to find her purpose and get past the damage done by irresponsible and cruel men.

But that was something to ponder another time. Another day. Now, she had a job to get to. People who counted on her and appreciated her. Two things she hadn't experienced in a really long time. Both might be small tokens to someone else, sentiments that were taken for granted or cast aside in favor of complaints about aching feet and hatred of washing dirty dishes.

Not to her. They gave her life purpose. Filled her with pride and satisfaction and the knowledge that she was more than the men in her life had made her believe. She was worth a damn, and she'd never forget that again.

COLD AIR BLASTED from the overhead vents in Cade Sulley's office. The chill fought against the oppressive heat trying to seep inside, but he didn't have time to focus on either. He scanned the columns of the spreadsheet his business partner, Matthew Metcalf, had sent over. The financial report didn't make a lick of sense.

A rap at the door lifted his head. Matthew stood in the doorway, a bemused smirk on his lips. "Looks like your head's about to explode."

Cade snorted. "Numbers, man. I freaking hate numbers."

He shifted his laptop so Matthew could see the computer screen.

Matthew laughed and plopped down on the lone chair in front of the desk. "That's why I do the finances, you manage the job sites."

"Fair point." Cade pinched the bridge of his nose and flipped the computer back toward him. Columns and rows littered the screen, adding up figures and projections of past projects.

"And luckily I can handle those finances while I'm out of town."

"Excuse me?" With his head pounding, Cade swiveled away from his computer and stared at his business partner.

Matthew had been his best friend since they were kids. They'd spent countless hours in the woods, building treehouses and looking for ways to stay out of trouble. A little mischief might have found them, but the creative hours spent using their hands and brains had led them to owning a construction company. A career where both of their strengths were used.

Matthew smiled wide, showcasing the dimples in his baby face. "I know it's last minute, but something's come up."

Cade frowned and waited for more information. "How long will you be gone?"

"Not sure. Brandon and I need to handle something."

"Handle something? Right before starting a new job that's just as important to us as it is to our community?"

"Sorry, can't be helped. But no worries. I thought I'd ask Laura to help with things in the office. Give her a chance to make some money. And who knows, maybe it can lead to something more stable for her. We're always bitching about needing to hire someone else around here."

The muscles in his gut clenched. Being in close quarters with Matthew's baby sister was a horrible idea, but he couldn't exactly tell his friend why. If he confessed how much he wanted to be near Laura, it'd surely result in a punch to the face. "We need help from someone who knows how to do the job. Not someone looking for a handout from family."

The lines in Matthew's face tightened. "A handout? Seriously?"

Cade winced and lifted his palms. "I meant we need someone who can step in and do the work. Not someone who's never been in this environment and will need tons of training. I don't have time for that."

Matthew moved his jaw back and forth. "She's smart, and she can help with the numbers and around the office while I'm gone. When I get back, we can discuss if it makes sense long term. If you don't think so, I won't push."

They could discuss Laura's place in the company as much as Matthew wanted, it wouldn't change Cade's mind. He'd made it a point to keep as far out of Laura Metcalf's path as possible in recent years.

When he'd joined the Army right out of high school, Laura was just an annoying kid who always followed him around. She'd been gangly with stringy blond hair and giant blue eyes too big for her face. But when he'd left the service, he'd found a grown-ass woman who took his breath away.

One who was more forbidden than the juiciest apple in creation.

Not only was she ten years his junior, but Matthew would kill him if he had any idea the kinds of thoughts that coursed through his mind any time he saw her.

Then there was her asshole of a boyfriend.

He fisted his hands on his thighs. He wasn't blind, nor was anyone else in town. He'd fought the urge to beat the abusive jerk into the ground numerous times, choosing to use his limited contact with Laura to offer kindness and reassurances instead. Useless gestures that didn't do a damn thing.

And now she carried the bastard's child. Heat flooded his veins, singeing his cheeks.

"Are you that upset about Laura working here while I'm gone?" Matthew asked, cutting into his thoughts. "I figured you'd be relieved. I swear, Laura's always been good with math and spreadsheets. She'll be a big help until I get back."

The subtle dip in Matthew's voice straightened his spine. "You and Brandon haven't left town since your honeymoon a couple years ago. What's going on?"

Dropping his gaze, Matthew shrugged then jumped to his feet. "Tell you if I could. Just know we have no other option but to go."

"When do you leave?"

Matthew checked the smart watch wrapped around his wrist. "About an hour."

"An hour?" Cade couldn't help the outburst of words. He and Matthew worked well together for several reasons, but open communication was number one. Now his buddy was leaving to do God knew what for God knew how long and tossing his sister in Cade's lap like a sexy grenade.

"I'll explain when I can. But for now, I've got to swing by the house, grab Brandon, and get the hell out of Dodge. Call if you need anything."

Cade's mouth hung open as his lifelong friend hurried out of the office.

A tiny twinge of irritation crawled up his spine, and he shut off his computer. Something wasn't right, but Matthew hadn't given him a chance to ask many questions. He had no choice but to trust his friend and whatever secrets he held.

Besides, he had a bigger problem. Keeping his distance from the one woman he could never, ever have—no matter how sweet the temptation.

2

The sugary scents of vanilla and cinnamon doughnuts wafted up Cade's nose and drew him closer to the brewing coffee in the corner of the reception area at Mountaintop Construction. His stomach growled, forcing him to grab a round glazed pastry. He sunk his teeth into the still-warm dough and groaned.

"I see you found the breakfast I brought in."

The soft feminine voice spun him around. Laura stood in the doorway with a shy smile, her blond hair pulled back into a low ponytail and minimal makeup on the delicate planes of her face. Not like she needed any goop to enhance her beauty, but in the years since Isaac's abuse had intensified, she was often seen with failed attempts at covering the bruises.

He forced the bite down his throat before setting the rest of his early morning treat on a stack of napkins Laura must have brought in as well. "You did this?"

"Is that okay? I wasn't sure what time you started work, so I got here bright and early to make sure everything was ready. Coffee's fresh, and I found some sugar and cream packets in the bottom draw of the reception desk." She tilted her head toward the neat-as-a-pin desk in the corner of the small room. "I can get something else if you prefer. Just tell me where it's kept."

Words tumbled out of her mouth, the pitch a tad higher than her normal voice.

He held up a palm to stop her and smiled. "This is perfect. Your brother pretends like he doesn't know how to work the machine, which leaves me to make coffee when I get in. And Lord knows there's never anything good to eat. Thank you."

She blew out a small breath, but the knotted hands in front of her waist told him not all of the anxiousness had left. Silence ebbed between them, the sound of the overworked air conditioning unit the only noise, and he rubbed the back of his neck. "So, any idea where Matthew and Brandon went?"

Frowning, she shook her head. "He didn't say. Only that he had to leave right away and would call when he could. He didn't mention anything to you?"

"Nope. Nothing."

"Weird."

More silence, the mounting tension hardening his jaw.

"Okay," he said, drawing out the word. This was one of the reasons why having Laura here was a mistake. They needed an employee who didn't stand there and stare at him with giant blue eyes that turned his insides to molten lava. One who could sit down, do her job, and not need direction.

Especially direction from him. He had a hard enough time getting his own shit together. He didn't need to be responsible for babysitting someone else. His job was to build things and oversee projects, not micromanage people. That'd been his job once before and it'd ended in a tragedy that had almost cost him his life.

Had cost the life of others.

She cleared her throat. "So what's first on your agenda?"

"Now that our bid has officially been accepted, I need to double check my measurements and make sure Mrs. Collins hasn't changed her mind about what she wants. Then I'll need to show her options for the materials needed for the remodel."

"Makes sense," she said, eyes wide as if absorbing his every word.

He glanced at his watch. "I have an appointment with Mrs. Collins at the pantry in about fifteen minutes."

"Can I go with you?" Laura asked.

He wanted to say no, to keep as much space between them as possible until it was time to send her on her way, but he couldn't. "Sure."

She beamed at him. "Perfect."

"Let me just put this coffee in a to-go cup and we can head out. It's only a couple blocks away." Steam billowed from the cup as he poured the bitter brew. The caffeine needed to pull double duty this morning—give him a jolt of energy and hopefully calm the anxiousness churning his gut.

Probably not possible but worth a try.

With the lid firmly in place, he pressed his lips together and turned back to Laura. "Let's go."

She met him at the door, which he pushed open for her then locked up behind them. The morning sun was already hot and blinding. He balled his fist at his side as he walked beside Laura. The floral scent of her perfume floated on the subtle breeze.

How was it possible she could smell so damn good? A wave of nostalgia slammed against him, messing with his head. She'd always picked flowers as a kid, passing them out to everyone she met throughout her day. He'd always shoved them in his pockets, only to find them hours later crumbled and broken.

He couldn't help but compare the flowers he'd once ignored and discarded to the woman Laura had become. Not because she wasn't strong and brave and incredible, but because she'd trusted her heart to a man who didn't deserve it—who'd tried to break her.

Just like he'd done with her sweet offerings of dandelions and lilacs.

"Have you ever been to the food pantry before?" he asked, needing to focus on the present instead of the past.

Laura stumbled over her feet.

He gripped her elbow to stabilize her and immediately regretted his actions. The feel of her soft skin sent a jolt of electricity through his veins. The side of her body brushed against his as she found her footing, and he bit back a groan before releasing her and taking a step away.

"Sorry," she said. "I'm always such a klutz."

Unable to speak from his suddenly dry mouth, he grunted a reply.

They reached the corner and turned away from the town square. The pantry was located close to downtown Pine Valley, but not in the middle of the mom-and-pop shops and tree-lined sidewalks. The standalone structure used to be a single-family home until it'd been turned into a community staple. A place for those down on their luck to get what they needed to help them.

"I've never been inside." Laura finally answered his question. "But I've always admired the outside. Wondered what it was like to live in such a beautiful Victorian home years ago when the town was first started. If those walls could talk, I'm sure there'd be tons of stories to be told."

He stared at her, admiring the wistful way she spoke about the gem of a structure he'd also loved. But the touch of sadness in her eyes twisted his gut. He wished he could comfort her. Could hold her in his arms and tell her everything would work out. But he didn't know that was true.

Not for her, and not for himself.

He stopped in front of the three-story house. White scalloped edging trimmed the roof and windows, setting off the buttercream and green siding. Bay windows combined with the wraparound porch and stunning turret told of another time, another era. "Some stories aren't meant to be retold."

The heat of her curious gaze bored into his cheek, but he kept his focus fixed ahead.

"I suppose you're right."

The crack in her voice turned him toward her. Her gaze stayed on his face, but the look in her eyes told him her mind was somewhere else.

Well, hell. He was off to a great start. He blew out a long breath, needing to get things back on track. "But new stories are always waiting to be discovered, and that's why I'm here. To help this place find a new tale to tell. New life, new meaning, new purpose. Or at least to add to the purpose it's always had."

Laura opened her mouth, but the front door burst open and an older woman with snow-white hair and glasses swept onto the porch, her smile wide and inviting. "Good morning."

Cade lifted a hand in greeting. "Morning, Mrs. Collins. I'm Cade Sulley with Mountaintop Construction."

Chuckling, she waved a hand through the air. "I've known who you are since you were knee-high to a grasshopper. And Laura Metcalf, so good to see you my dear. Please, come in."

He followed Laura up the old steps and walked inside. It was time to focus on work and block out all the other bullshit. This was an important job, and he couldn't let his mind wander.

Or let Laura Metcalf distract him any more than she already had.

~

THE BRIGHT LIGHT of the computer blurred Laura's eyes. She rubbed them, but the motion did nothing to take away the strain. She couldn't remember the last time she'd sat and stared at a screen for so many hours.

Probably never.

Even in high school, she'd skated by on the bare minimum effort. Half-assing assignments and skipping class to spend time with Isaac. He'd guilted her into stepping away from her comfort zone. Convinced her that she'd do things her heart told her was wrong if she truly loved him.

She'd been so young and desperate for love and affection. His scraps of kindness had lured her into a false sense of security until she'd been trapped, the thought of escape as much of a fantasy as the man she was chained to.

But not anymore. No more chains, no more beatings, no more lies. And now she'd prove herself to everyone around her and make her way in the world. Provide her child with the love and life she'd always wanted.

Heavy footsteps ambled down the hall, and she sat up straight. Her heart fluttered in her chest. Spending the day working with Cade hadn't gone how she'd expected, but it hadn't been horrible. They'd shared an interesting moment on their way to the food pantry then he'd kept his distance once they returned to the office. Probably busy making plans to help make Mrs. Collins' dreams come true.

Or avoiding her.

"Still at it?" he asked, stopping in front of her desk. The strap of his laptop bag hung on one shoulder, and he held a cluster of files in his hand. His dark hair was disheveled, as if he'd run his fingers through it a hundred times, and his constant five o'clock shadow enhanced his chiseled jawline.

With her fingers glued to the keyboard, she glanced up. "Yeah. I spent most of the day getting acquainted with your different systems and organizing things. Now I'm going over some of the numbers for the new project."

"You didn't have to do all that."

She shrugged. "To be honest, I wasn't exactly sure what to do."

He grimaced. "Sorry 'bout that. I guess I should have given you some direction."

"That's okay. I'm supposed to be making your life easier, not harder. I've gotten a good handle on how you guys operate, and I think I'll be able to help with the different aspects of payment with the pantry. It's a little different with money coming in from multiple avenues and not one source."

"Sounds like a pain in the ass."

"Which is why I'm taking on the numbers while you handle the planning." She nodded toward the jumble of papers spilling from the stack of files.

He placed his free hand over his heart. "My angel."

Heat crept up her neck at his compliment and she dropped her gaze. "Just doing my job." She inwardly cringed at the false cheerfulness in her voice. He made her so damn uneasy. Not in the way a lot of men did nowadays. In a way that reminded her that even after all her years suffering under Isaac's abusive thumb, she was still a woman.

A woman who couldn't help but appreciate a handsome and kind man.

Okay, enough. Cade was her brother's best friend. He was nice to her because of Matthew. Just like he'd put up with her traipsing after him in the woods and giving him treasures she'd found. She had to stop whatever silly childhood fancies still lingered in her head. Those were obviously purely a way to cling to a simpler time and forget her daily struggles.

Not a smart way to handle her issues.

Cade cleared his throat, a nervous tic she remembered he had as a kid. "Well, umm, I'm headed home. Why don't you do the same? I can wait and lock up after you."

Although tempted, she shook her head. "No, thanks. I found some papers shoved in the desk drawer I want to file and other odds and ends I'd like to sort before tomorrow. Then I can come in knowing I have everything the way I like it."

Her excuse may be complete bullshit, but there was no reason for Cade to question it. Besides, sounding like an over-achiever was better than admitting how much she hated to be home. To sit in a tiny house night after night lost in her fears about her future.

He gave a sharp nod. "All right then. I'll see you in the morning."

She offered him a smile and waited for him to leave before hanging her head on a sigh. The offer to work for her brother's construction company had seemed like an amazing opportunity, but now she wasn't so sure. The weird tension she felt when around Cade was exhausting, if not the teensiest bit exciting. But she wasn't at a point in her life where she could afford to focus on anything other than her baby.

Which is why staying late and figuring out what she could do to make herself invaluable here was important.

Switching gears, she opened the top drawer of the desk and grabbed the crumbled paperwork. She tried to remember if Matthew had ever had a secretary, but she couldn't think of anyone.

Not like she'd spent much time in the office or talking to her brother about his business. She'd been too caught up in her nightmare. But whoever had sat in this desk chair last had been a mess. Wanting things as neat as possible, she flattened the wrinkled papers then found their proper homes in the large wooden filing cabinet behind the desk. Now to clean the clutter and wipe out the dirt. Then she'd head home.

Sitting back down on the squeaky chair, she picked out wadded up post-it notes and bent paper clips. She swiped her hand along the smooth wood and the tips of her fingers brushed against something small and hard trapped at the far corner at the back of the drawer. Determined to clean every last inch of the desk, she tugged on the object until she pulled out a flash drive.

"Hmm, what's this doing in there?" She flipped the rectangular device between her fingers.

Intrigued, she found the correct slot in the computer and shoved it in.

Thud!

The loud blast of sound coming from down the hall set her nerves on edge—like a tree branch whacking against a window.

She stilled, holding her breath and tuning into every shift of energy in the air. Goosebumps skittered up her arms. Her heart pumped like crazy in her chest.

Time to go. Being alone in the unfamiliar space was clearly messing with her head. She'd shut down for the night, go home, and cuddle on the couch with a soft blanket and leftovers from the night before. Maybe put on a comedy to clear away the ridiculous cloud of dread that had settled over her.

She waited another beat to make sure nothing came shooting down the hall, then quickly turned off the computer and gathered her things. With her keys in hand, she headed for the door.

Swift footsteps reached her ears in seconds. She bolted toward the front entrance without looking back. She'd spent enough years running from danger to recognize that something was wrong. She grabbed the doorknob with her free hand and yanked open the door.

A hard body came up behind her and slammed the door shut. A heavy hand dug into her shoulder.

She opened her mouth and screamed.

3

The evening air hadn't cooled much. Cade breathed in deep, glad to finally be out of the office—even if only a few steps away. Day one working with Laura was finished, and Lord only knew how many more left.

He'd text Matthew when he got home and demand answers. They were partners and this secrecy crap wasn't acceptable.

Not with basic questions like where are you and when are you coming back.

With one decision made, his growling stomach forced his attention to another.

Dinner.

After filling up on doughnuts, he'd skipped lunch. He could drive home and cook for himself, but that'd take far too long. Besides, he hadn't been to the grocery store in almost a week and his fridge was bare. Much better to head to the Chill N' Grill and grab a burger. Maybe even a cold beer to wash away the lingering knots in his stomach.

A pang of guilt stopped his progress to his truck parked on

the side of the road. Laura hadn't touched the doughnuts, and she hadn't left for lunch either.

Had she packed something to eat?

The mini-fridge he kept stocked with soda hadn't held any signs of a homemade lunch. Matthew didn't talk much about his family, but Cade had heard enough whispers around town to understand Laura's situation.

A situation that was tough with only herself to look after, let alone a baby on the way. And she'd used what little resources she had to buy him breakfast. Which he'd scarfed down with a quick thanks and no second thought.

Dammit. He should offer to take her with him for dinner. Make sure she had something to eat and thank her for all the help today. It really was the least he could do.

A panicked scream cut through the muggy night and made his pulse jump at his throat.

Laura!

He sprinted back to the office and yanked on the door. It didn't budge. He fisted his hand and pounded on the thick wood. "Laura! It's Cade! Open the door!"

Dull thuds and shuffling feet reached his ears and he dug into his pocket for his keys. He unlocked the deadbolt with shaky hands and shoved open the door.

Laura curled in the fetal position on the floor in the corner. Sobs shaking her shoulders and tears streaming down her face. Her arms were cradled around her abdomen.

Oh God. The baby.

He dropped to her side and reached for her.

She flinched and curled even tighter into herself.

A ball of anger lodged in his throat. He kept his hands on his thighs, struggling not to smooth back her hair or wipe the moisture from her face. Anything to show her she was safe with him. "It's okay, Laura. I'm not going to hurt you. I just want to make sure you're okay and find out what happened."

"There was someone in here." She sniffed back more tears and closed her eyes. "I heard a noise and got spooked. I decided to leave. Hurried to the door, but when I cracked it open, someone slammed it shut. He grabbed me, and I screamed."

Fury raged inside him. "Did you see the person? Know them?" He debated asking if Isaac had followed her to work and waited for him to leave before attacking, but that asshole was suspect number one in his mind no matter the answer.

She shook her head. "You pounded on the door so quick. I think it scared him. He threw me on the ground and ran out the back. I only saw him from behind, but he was dressed all in black. A knit hat around his head."

Cade wanted to sprint down the darkened hallway. Maybe he'd have a chance to run back there and catch whoever'd done this. But a light touch on his hand rooted him to the spot.

With one palm still snug around her stomach, she squeezed his hand. "I landed hard, face first on the ground."

The fresh bout of tears and hitch in her voice broadcasted her fear louder than any words she could have said. He tightened his jaw, determined to keep both Laura and her baby safe. He dug his phone from his pocket. "You're both going to be fine, okay? I'm going to call the sheriff so they can find who did this. I'll tell them to bring an ambulance. I'm sure there's nothing to worry about, but a quick trip to the hospital will make everyone feel better."

She nodded and tightened her grip on his hand.

Struggling not to let the soft feel of her palm mess with his head, he dialed the local sheriff's department and described what had happened to the dispatcher.

"Someone will be here soon," he told Laura as he disconnected. "Is there anyone else you want me to call?"

A flash of hesitation lingered in her eyes and a few seconds passed before she answered. "No."

The admission crushed him. If he'd been hurt or scared, he

had an army of people to surround him. Too many, actually, but his large family always meant well. Even if their support could be suffocating at times.

"Do you want to stand?" he asked. "Or get onto a chair?"

She bit her bottom lip then nodded.

He stood first then leaned forward to cup her elbow under one hand while bracing her back with the other, helping her to her feet. He watched every muscle in her face for any signs of distress or pain. "Does anything hurt?"

"My side," she said, voice small. "I tried to pivot when he pushed me so I didn't land on the baby."

He forced a small smile. "You're already the mother of the year. Looking out for that kiddo."

That coaxed a grin from her, transforming her red-nosed puffy face into the look of a proud mother.

"Let's get you in one of the chairs to relax." He helped her settle into the cushioned seat in front of the desk. "Can I get you anything? Water?"

"Can you just sit with me? I...I don't want to be alone."

He swallowed hard, hating how much she was hurting. How frightened she was.

Because he'd left her here alone.

Never again. Until they got to the bottom of what had happened, he'd make sure she was safe. While he stood watch, no one would ever get their hands on her again.

THE GRAINY BLOB on the silky square paper stared back at Laura. She wanted to grasp the tiny reminder that her baby was okay all night, but instead she used a magnet to stick it to the cream-colored refrigerator.

Relief trickled through her veins. She rested a palm on her belly. Fearing for the life of her unborn child had been the scariest moment she'd ever experienced. And since her life had been far from rainbows and butterflies, that said a lot.

The crinkling of paper food bags turned her toward the two-person table in her tiny kitchen. Cade set out take-out boxes and napkins. The smell of greasy burgers and French fries made her mouth water.

"You didn't need to order all this food. I already made you stay with me at the hospital while they checked me over. This is too much."

"First, you didn't make me do anything. I wanted to be with you. Doesn't matter why a doc's lookin' you over, it's scary as hell. Add in the baby and it's downright terrifying. And second, if I was starving, you had to be too." He grabbed a large, clear bowl and set it next to her burger. "Got you a salad, too."

She wrinkled her nose.

"Not a fan?" he chuckled and crossed the kitchen to the sink.

"Not when I have a burger staring me in the face."

"Fair point. Go ahead and get started. Glasses in here?" He tilted his chin toward the cabinet to his left.

She nodded.

"Water okay? I would have ordered you something to drink at the restaurant, but I know pregnant women aren't supposed to have caffeine, and booze is a no go."

Amused, she watched him gather two tall glasses and fill them with water from the tap before sitting in the chair across from her. "How do you know what pregnant women aren't allowed to have?"

"I have three sisters. Two have kids, and both like to overshare."

"Oh, that's right. That was a dumb question. I should have known better." Heat slammed against her cheeks. She took the offered glass and swallowed a large sip before focusing her downcast eyes on the untouched burger.

As hungry as she'd been, suddenly the thought of taking a bite of anything made her instantly nauseous.

"Not a dumb question at all. It's been years since my sisters were in town. No reason for you to remember them."

She offered a tight smile but couldn't make herself stare past the box of untouched food in front of her. "Did you tell Wade who the extra meal was for?" she asked, changing the subject.

"Nah. Didn't figure it was his business."

Letting out a small breath, she finally met his eye. "Thank you."

The owner of the Chill N' Grill wasn't just the man who helped her out by letting her work shifts. He was her sister's fiancé. Throughout all the years when her sister had been gone, Wade had always been her champion.

Even when she'd pushed him away. Just like she pushed away every person who'd shown her concern or voiced an opinion she didn't want to hear.

But as much as she loved and appreciated Wade, she didn't want him to know what had happened tonight. And she definitely didn't want him telling Jude.

Cade took a bite of his burger then set it down before taking a sip of water. "Do you want to talk about what happened?"

She closed her eyes, replaying her latest nightmare.

"You don't have to," he said. "You've told the police and replayed it at the hospital when talking to your doctor. I want you to know I'm here, too."

The gentle timbre of his voice cracked something inside her. Tears pricked the corners of her eyes. She could brace herself against judgment and anger and even violence. His kindness was what disarmed her.

Summoning her courage, she focused on him and the compassion pouring off him in waves. "I've been scared many times before in my life, but this was different."

He frowned and pushed aside his food. "How so?"

"I didn't see it coming. Didn't know who was attacking me. Didn't know why it was happening."

"Are you sure you didn't know the person?"

The question was like a slap in the face, and one she'd asked herself countless times. "I guess I can't be sure."

"Was there anything familiar about him? A smell? Anything?"

The deputy had asked her the same questions and she had the same answer now as she did then. "Nothing."

Cade ran a hand over his finger-length hair. "Would Isaac show up and do this? I mean, nothing in the office was touched. Nothing taken. The video surveillance shows someone breaking in through the window, coming straight for you, then leaving when I arrived."

"But why would he dress in black? Cover his head in a ski mask and hands in gloves? He's never hidden himself when coming after me before. Why would he now?"

Cade grabbed a fry and took a bite as if chewing the question over along with his food. "Maybe to mess with your head. A way to get back at you for leaving. How does he feel about the baby?"

The mention of her child brought her hand to her abdomen. "We haven't talked about it. I don't want anything to do with him, and I want him far away from my baby."

"I don't blame you, but he might have other plans."

She blew out a shaky breath. Leaving Isaac had been the hardest thing she'd ever done. No way in hell would she ever subject her child to such a cruel man.

"I don't want to scare you." Cade lifted his palms as if to reassure her. "I'm laying out some options. The police were going to question him. Not sure if it's better or worse to find out he's not the guy we're after."

She cringed, a different kind of fear settling over her. "What happens now? We sit around and wait for the police? Or worse, wait for him to attack again?" Just her luck. She'd finally run from her captor only for some other madman to swoop in and steal her very precarious sense of security.

"I don't think there's any other choice. Is there somewhere you can stay—someone who can stay with you—until we have more answers? Just as a precaution."

Going back to her parents' house wasn't an option, and no way her father would allow her mother to stay with her for an entire night. She still wasn't completely comfortable around Jude, and the closest friend she'd made in the last couple years was visiting Colorado with the man she loved and his two little girls.

Hating to admit it, she shook her head. "Matthew is the one I'd call, but he's not around."

Pity swam in his green eyes, making her already uneasy stomach even more upset. She didn't want his, or anyone else's, sympathy. She was strong and capable. "I'll be fine," she lied. "I have locks on my door and it's a good neighborhood. Besides, the person probably doesn't even know where I live."

Cade shifted in his chair, clearly not convinced. "How about I stick around a little while longer? We can finish our meal and maybe watch some TV. Once you're too tired to be scared, I'll leave. Sound good?"

The tension bunching the muscles in her neck loosened. She hated to admit how much she wanted him to stay, but agreeing to such a sensible plan was only logical. "Okay. As long as you let me pick the show."

"Deal."

Plan made, she nibbled on a fry. Her appetite still wavered, but she needed food in her system. Besides, keeping her meal down was the least of her worries. She'd have to figure out how to be alone eventually, no matter who was out to get her.

4

The television droned on, sucking Cade into the storyline despite the shitstorm brewing in his mind. He kept his phone clutched in one hand and willed it to ring. The noose of tension wringing his neck wouldn't loosen until he had more answers.

Answers about the break-in. Answers about where the hell Matthew was—seriously, how could the guy not call back after his sister had been attacked? Answers about Isaac's whereabouts during the time Laura had been terrorized.

But the dark phone screen stared back at him in silent mockery.

He chanced a peek at Laura. She sat on the opposite end of the sofa, her feet tucked beneath her, and a blanket draped across her lap. She'd changed from her pencil skirt and loose-fitting blouse to black leggings and an oversized T-shirt.

A large bowl of half-eaten popcorn sat between them on the worn, gray cushion. He hadn't touched it, but Laura's hand returned to the buttery kernels time and time again while her eyes stayed glued to the mustached soccer coach on the screen.

Cade was more than happy to watch her fill her stomach and zone out. Hopefully some of the stress would melt away.

Her phone glowed from its spot on the end table, heightening his stress level by ten notches.

Laura's body stiffened, and she caught his eye. "Unknown number."

"Answer it." He scooted forward on the couch, forearms on knees.

A tiny tremor shook her hand as she scooped up her phone and accepted the call then quickly activated the speaker so Cade could hear. "Hello," she said, placing the device between them.

"Good evening. This is Deputy Owen Wells. Am I speaking with Laura Metcalf?"

"Yes."

Cade leaned closer so he wouldn't miss a word just as Laura moved toward the middle of the sofa, as if needing his support.

"I wanted to touch base and let you know we spoke with Isaac Heck. He has an alibi for the time in question."

Cade worked his clenched jaw back and forth. He was confident the deputy had done his job, but Isaac was a slippery sonofabitch.

"Oh, okay," Laura stammered.

"Is there anyone else I should speak with? Anyone else who might want to hurt you?"

She shook her head, tears gathering in her eyes. "Not that I can think of."

"If that changes, please give me a call. Until we speak again, be safe. I'll make sure we have a squad car patrol your neighborhood for the time being. But until we know exactly who attacked you and why, you can't be too careful."

"Thank you, Deputy." She disconnected and stared into the distance, shock clear on her open mouth and wide eyes.

"Hey, now. Everything's going to be okay." Wanting to

comfort her, Cade placed the popcorn bowl on the coffee table and sat beside her. He hooked an arm on the top of the couch above her shoulders, mindful not to touch her but needing to be close.

"How can you say that? The only person I know who hates me enough to hurt me has an alibi. What does that mean? Does someone else have issues with me? Was I just in the wrong place at the wrong time? How do I step outside and not fear someone not even on my radar is going to fly at me out of nowhere?"

The crack in her voice constricted his chest. "I don't know why this happened. You don't deserve it. But you have an entire town of people who love you and want the best for you. We'll all stand with you until we get to the bottom of this."

She hung her head, unmoved.

"Do you feel unsafe working for Mountaintop Construction?" He held his breath waiting for an answer. As much as he'd fought against the idea of her working for him and Matthew, the thought of her not coming back the next day was more upsetting than it should be.

She chewed her bottom lip, gaze still focused ahead. "I want to say no. I really need the job. But sitting in that reception area all by myself will make me nervous. I'm not sure I can do it."

"I understand. What if there's a way to keep working for us without being alone? Without feeling exposed or vulnerable?"

She finally looked at him, brows raised.

Great. Now he had to come up with an idea quick that didn't involve him being chained to her side for the foreseeable future. Not like that sounded all bad.

Dammit, focus.

"What if I talk to Mrs. Collins about setting you up at the food pantry? You can work from there and never have to be alone. I'll be spending most of my time there soon anyway, and even when I'm not around, you'll never be by yourself."

She tilted her head to the side like an interested puppy. "How can I do work for the construction company at the pantry?"

"Most of what we need you to do can be done on the computer. You can do it anywhere, really. And if I'm onsite, you can help me whenever I have issues Matthew usually deals with. Managing employees, being the point person in charge of speaking with Mrs. Collins about project updates, even helping with design plans if that's something you're interested in."

Finally, her eyes lit. "You'd let me do all that?"

He shrugged. "Why not?"

A deep frown suddenly erased all her joy. "Will my being there put Mrs. Collins and the other volunteers at risk?"

"At this point, we don't know why the break-in occurred. It might not have anything to do with you. But I'll be transparent with Mrs. Collins and make sure she's comfortable with everything."

"That sounds perfect." Her last word was interrupted by a yawn. "Sorry, it's been a long day."

He smiled. "No apologies necessary. Besides, it's getting late. You should get to sleep. Will you be all right here alone?"

"Yes. Deputy Wells is having the area patrolled throughout the night and I'll lock up behind you. I'll keep my pepper spray and phone by my bed just in case."

A subtle tug of disappointment weighed down his gut. He ignored it and stood. "I'll get out of your hair then. You have my number, right?"

She nodded.

"Call if you need anything. No matter the issue or time."

She offered the tiniest glimpse of a smile. "Okay. And thanks for dinner."

"Anytime." He shoved his hands in the pockets of his trousers so he wouldn't do anything stupid then dipped his chin before heading to the door. "I'll wait on the porch to make sure you lock up before I leave."

She jumped to her feet and hurried behind him. "Good idea. You've been great all night. Seriously. I don't know what I would have done without you."

He hesitated in the doorway for a beat, unable to tear himself from her. She was so close, her warm breath skimmed his cheek. All he had to do was lean down and brush his lips to hers. It'd be so easy, so simple, so....

She rested a hand on her barely-there baby bump and snapped him back to the moment. The last thing she needed was someone making inappropriate advances when she was in a vulnerable situation. Especially not him.

Never him.

Clearing his throat, he stepped into the night. Stars twinkled above him, the outline of the mountains a mere shadow between towering maples and full evergreens. He listened for the click of the locks then hustled to his truck parked in front of her house.

With his nerves zipping with enough energy to power the entire town, he hopped into the driver's seat and stared at the little house nestled amongst the row of old homes. The living room light clicked off.

Good, she was going to bed.

He didn't want to leave her, didn't want to think of her alone and defenseless. He shifted against the smooth leather, getting as comfortable as possible. He'd stay a little while longer. Until his gut told him it was okay to head home.

But until then, he'd stand guard.

WARM RAYS of sunshine filtered through the window in Laura's room and fell across her face. She grimaced. For the love of

God, her alarm hadn't even gone off yet. She really needed to buy curtains for her house. It might not be the home she dreamed of, but a bit of sprucing might make it a little cozier.

She simply needed to find the money to spruce.

Which meant she should get out of bed—alarm off or not—and get ready for work.

The memories of her first day of work crashed down on her, forcing her to burrow back under her thin covers. The terror of the evening was almost forgotten due to the comfortable night she'd spent with Cade.

Almost.

No matter how nice it'd been to munch on microwave popcorn and watch a feel-good comedy with a handsome man on her couch, it couldn't erase the attack. Or the fact she had no idea who'd gone after her or why.

Bang! Bang! Bang!

Heavy pounding slammed against the front door.

She groaned and pulled her pillow over her head, still half asleep. This wasn't how she wanted to start her day. Roused from bed by some aggressive stranger when she should have twenty more minutes to sleep. Since leaving Isaac, it was the little luxuries that meant the most to her. Lounging in bed on her phone before taking a long, hot shower then eating whatever she had on hand for breakfast.

For years she'd hurried from bed in the wee hours to have coffee brewed and a meal fit for a king on the table before her ex had even cracked an eyelid. She'd learned fast to do everything she could to put him in a good mood to increase her chance of making it through the day without another slap.

But even that hadn't worked.

Bang! Bang!

Alarm finally set in, and she grabbed her phone. Had someone tried to call, and she hadn't woken? Maybe they found her attacker.

No missed calls.

Irritated and exhausted, she jumped out of bed, yanked her robe from the hook on her door, and stomped down the hall. She opened the door.

Isaac took a step forward and glared down at her. A snarl turned his angel-like face into the devil himself. "What the hell do you think you're doing?"

Tremors took over her body. Fear paralyzed her and transported her right back to the meek woman she'd been in his presence.

He pounded his fist on the door inches from her head. "Answer me. Why did you send deputies to my house? Like I'm some kind of criminal. I work for your father in the mayor's office for God's sake. Do you know how that makes me look?"

Spit flew from his mouth and landed on her cheek, snapping her from her terror-induced stupor. She tried to scurry behind the door, but he clamped down on her wrist and pulled her forward. The belt around her robe loosened, the material revealing the subtle bump under her sleep tank.

Isaac's brown eyes widened, and he tightened his grip. "So, the rumors around town are true for once. Were you ever going to tell me I'm going to be a daddy?"

She cradled her abdomen with her free arm. "You'll never see this child."

His snarl slid into a smirk that made bile shoot up her throat. "You think you can stop me? You've always been a silly girl, but I never knew you were so freaking stupid. No one will stop me from seeing my kid. If anything, you should be worried about people thinking you're an unfit mother. Everyone knows what a screwup you are."

A nearby slamming car door rang in her ears, mixed with the panicked buzzing in her brain. She fought to keep herself steady. To not cower under his threats.

But were they real? Could he declare her unfit and take her child?

He could try, but she'd fight with her dying breath to keep him away.

"Is there a problem?"

Isaac glanced over his shoulder, giving her a glimpse of a very pissed off Cade marching through the grass. Seeing his face sent a wave of relief so intense crashing over her, she almost fell over.

"What the hell do you want?" Isaac barked the question but released her wrist.

Bullies always back down when in the face of someone stronger. Someone bigger. Someone better.

Cade was all of those things and more.

"I want to know why you're harassing Laura." Cade didn't slow his pace until he took the three steps, crossed the porch, and stopped at her side.

He had a good four inches on Isaac. His broad chest and muscled arms made him far more intimidating, especially once her slimy ex fixed his fake as shit smile on his face.

The smile he used to charm anyone and everyone.

The smile she'd fallen hard for, before she'd learned it was a mask to trick and manipulate.

"I'm just talking to the mother of my child and wondering why she'd ever think I'd break into a local business to harm her. I don't see how that's any of your concern." His anger at the interruption caused a little of his annoyance to slip through the cracks of his façade.

Cade stood tall beside her, making her straighten her spine and lift her chin. She met Isaac dead in the eyes. "He's my friend and has way more reason to be here than you. We have nothing to discuss, so I suggest you leave my property. Now."

Isaac laughed, the sound like broken glass. "Big brave girl now, huh? You won't be so brave when your *friend* isn't around."

The truth behind the taunt stung, but she wouldn't let him see how much his words affected her.

"Is that a threat?" Cade crossed his arms over his chest, making him appear even bigger.

Isaac glared then stalked back to his car.

Watching him drive away, Laura melted against Cade. The feel of his strong body kept her steady and slowed her frantic heart rate. This was a man who wanted to keep her safe, protect her.

Never hurt her.

Coming to her senses, she straightened and put some space between them. No, this was Cade. Her brother's best friend, who was stepping in to help her. Same thing he'd do for anyone.

She smoothed a hand over her messy hair and cringed. "Thanks for that, but what are you doing here?"

Pink tinged his cheeks. Rubbing the back of his neck, his gaze dropped to the floor. "I slept in my truck."

"What?"

"Didn't feel right leaving you. I planned to stay for a few minutes and kind of fell asleep."

The bashful expression pinching his face warmed her core. He'd spent the entire night crammed in his truck to make sure she was safe.

Besides Matthew—who'd always had his own issues—no one had looked out for her. Never put her needs above their own. She studied the slight crook in his nose and the intensity of his green eyes. The boy she'd once held a childhood crush on was now the most handsome man she'd ever seen. Her breath stalled in her chest.

Oh boy. Cade brought with him a different kind of trouble.

A kind of trouble that could hurt her worse than anything ever had before.

5

The crick in Cade's neck screamed as he pulled into his driveway and parked. He didn't have much time, but no way he could show up for work in yesterday's rumpled clothes and unbrushed teeth.

Not to mention that anger still shook his veins from his encounter with Isaac. It'd taken all his self-control not to slam his fist in the asshole's face. But that wouldn't have made the situation better for Laura. If anything, it would have made it worse.

So instead he'd watched the other man slink away then waited for Laura to get ready for the day before bringing them both back to his place.

"I've never seen your house before." Laura peered out the passenger side window. "It's lovely."

Pride puffed his chest as he climbed down from his truck and waited for her to step outside. "Thanks," he said, leading the way to the wide porch that wrapped around his cabin. The morning sun leaked through the trees covering his property. He took a second to pause on the carefully laid brick pathway and breathe in the mountain air, grateful for the sanctuary he'd built with his own two hands. "This place saved me."

Laura stopped beside him and stared up with raised brows. Nothing but pure curiosity on her face. "How so?"

He struggled to find the words to explain how using his hands to build something pure and good had transformed him after returning from the military to civilian life. Speaking about the nightmare he'd walked through wasn't easy for him—hell, he'd never even spoken with Matthew about the part he'd played in the deaths of his brothers in arms. How could he explain it to Laura without sharing too much—without exposing secrets he planned to take to his deathbed?

A gentle touch on his arm broke through his darkening thoughts. "You don't have to tell me anything you're not comfortable sharing."

The quiet compassion in her voice softened his walls. He settled on the porch steps and stared out at the beginning of a beautiful new day. Birds chirped nearby and a subtle breeze brushed his cheeks. He wanted to open up a little, to show her there's a way forward after the shit hit the fan.

"Nah, it's okay. I just don't talk about it much." He snorted. "Not at all really. I'm sure that's not the healthiest way to deal with my issues. But if talking was my thing, then I wouldn't have this. I wouldn't have a successful business where I do what I love."

Staying quiet, she sat and left an inch of space between them.

When the silence stretched on, he continued. "When I came home, I was a wreck. My mind, my nerves, my everything. I'd wanted out of Army life for so long, but when I came back to Pine Valley, I didn't belong. Didn't have a place here anymore like I had before. Add in PTSD and a ton of other shit I won't get into, and I was lost."

"How'd you find yourself again?"

"Your brother stepped in." Matthew might be pissing him off right now, but Cade smiled at the memory of his best friend swooping in and helping get his life back on track. "He found me drunk at the bar and laid into me. He didn't pussyfoot around, didn't offer pity or sympathy. He gave me exactly what I needed—told me exactly what I needed to hear."

Laura turned to him. Her head tilted to the side so her long blond hair spilled over one shoulder. "Which was?"

"To get off my ass. To get out of my head for a bit and start using my hands. To go back to my roots and do what I loved. So I bought this little patch of land outside of town and some tools and just started building. Every day, I came here and sweated out my anger and fears and troubles as best I could. And every day your brother worked beside me."

"Sounds like Matthew."

He nodded his agreement. "He didn't save me, but he helped me save myself. Gave me purpose when I was drowning. And because of that, Mountaintop Construction was born, and I had a new home to live in."

She sighed and propped her chin on her fist. "Sounds like you figured out how to take something painful and turn it into something beautiful."

He studied her profile. He wanted to run his finger along the gentle slope of her nose or sweep the long strands of unruly hair behind her ear.

Get it together man.

Forcing his gaze forward, he focused on the wistful tone of her words. "I did, and you can too."

She rested a palm on her tiny bump. "I hope so."

The visual reminder of what her future held was like a fist in the gut. She had so much on her plate, the last thing she needed was for him to sit beside her with a headful of inappropriate thoughts. She needed a friend now more than anything else, and he needed to remember that, or he'd kick his own ass.

"I have no doubt." He hopped up and offered her a hand. "Do you want to step inside while I change?"

She nestled her palm in his.

He couldn't resist skimming the pad of his thumb across her smooth skin before pulling her to her feet.

Her subtle inhale of breath clenched his stomach muscles.

He dropped her hand and headed for the door. He might be late for work, but before he could continue his day with Laura by his side, he needed to take an ice-cold shower.

LAURA SQUARED her shoulders and lifted her chin as she stepped into Mountaintop Construction's office. The day was young, but between her confrontation with Isaac and time spent in Cade's house while he showered, her nerves were stretched so tight she swore she'd snap any second.

Now she had to face the place where she'd been attacked, left on the floor like a pile of trash.

"You sure you're okay?" Cade asked as if sensing her unease. He closed and locked the door behind him.

She stood near the entrance and stared down at the spot where she'd curled into herself, afraid she'd lost the baby. She closed her eyes and sucked in a deep breath. The baby was fine. She was fine.

A touch on her shoulder turned her around. She found herself gazing into Cade's concerned eyes. "It's hard thinking about what happened, but I'm all right."

He flattened his lips into a thin line. "I have to grab a few things, and I'd like to take a closer look to make sure nothing was tampered with. Nothing taken. If you'd like, I can walk you down to the food pantry to hang out with Mrs. Collins while I do a quick search."

"Don't be silly. I can help you. That's what you're paying me for, right?" She forced a lightness to her voice that rang false in her own ears. And judging by the way Cade scrunched his nose, he didn't buy it either.

A soft knock on the door spared her from keeping her foot in her mouth.

Cade frowned and glanced past her. "Looks like your sister's here."

Dread and excitement combatted in the pit of her stomach. Complicated didn't even scratch the surface when describing her relationship with Jude. She'd loved her sister more than life when she'd been younger, but when she'd left town, it had been the beginning of Laura's belief that she wasn't good enough to keep the people she loved around.

A brutal lesson drilled into her by her father any chance he got.

"Do you want me to let her in?" Cade hesitated with his hand on the doorknob.

She sighed. After Jude's brush with death months before, she'd stayed in town and had been working on rebuilding relationships with those she'd left behind. Laura loved having Jude back in her life, but a few walls still remained where her sister was concerned. "Sure."

Cade unlocked the door, and Jude burst inside. She'd cut her blond locks to sit at her shoulders. Worry and fear tightened the lines of her face. She stopped short of wrapping her arms around Laura, as if instinctively knowing the physical affection would be too much for her.

"I heard what happened. Are you hurt? Is the baby okay?" Clasping her hands in front of her, Jude flicked her gaze to Laura's belly.

Laura cradled her bump. "We're both fine. Just a little shaken. How'd you know something happened?"

Jude shrugged. "You know how small towns are. Can't keep secrets for long. Not to mention Isaac's already been all over this morning proclaiming his innocence and outrage at being questioned."

Heat crept up Laura's cheeks. Pine Valley was a great place to live until she was the center of attention—something that happened more often than she liked.

"Prick," Cade muttered, gaining both her and Jude's attention.

Jude quirked a light eyebrow.

"You heard me," Cade said. "Isaac's a prick."

"Couldn't agree more, but was he the one who broke in here last night?" Jude asked.

Suddenly exhausted, Laura slunk around the desk and slumped down in the leather rolling chair. "Who knows? I couldn't see the person, but it's strange to think he'd hide himself if he wanted to hurt me. He never has before."

Jude winced and Cade tightened his hands to fists at his side.

"But he was pissed this morning," she said, pressing on despite their reactions. "Claimed he had an alibi, which he gave to the deputy who questioned him."

Frowning, Jude took a step forward. "What do you mean he was pissed this morning?"

"He showed up at my house."

"What?" Jude shook her head, rage clear in her every movement.

Laura lifted a hand to calm her. "It was fine. Cade was there and took care of everything."

Jude's jaw hung open for a second before she snapped it shut and aimed narrowed eyes at Cade. "Oh really?"

Cade rubbed the back of his neck and scrunched up his nose.

A different kind of heat slammed against Laura's cheeks. Jude wouldn't spread gossip about her around town, but best to make it clear there was nothing beyond friendship between her and Cade. "He slept in his truck. It was no big deal."

Cade worked his jaw back and forth then cleared his throat. "I'll let you two talk while I search the office and gather what I need before heading to the pantry."

Jude stared after him, only glancing back at Laura once he'd disappeared down the hall. "Why'd he sleep in his truck?"

"To make sure I was safe. He planned to stay for a few minutes and fell asleep."

"Awe, that's sweet." Jude skirted around the chair situated in front of the desk and sat. "He was always like a second big brother to us."

Laura nearly choked on the lump forming in her throat. Even if the stupid attraction pulling her to Cade was due to his kindness, it definitely wasn't something she'd feel for a brother. But that was beside the point.

"He can't keep sleeping in his truck. Why don't you stay with me and Wade?" Jude asked. "At least until we know what's going on."

"In that tiny studio apartment above the bar? Sounds cozy."

Jude swished her lips to the side. "We could stay with you? Or I could. We could make it fun. Like when you were little. Pizza, movies, milkshakes. The whole nine yards."

More conflicting emotions duked it out inside Laura. She didn't want to be a burden on the people around her, but she also didn't want to be alone tonight. Cade had been sweet to spend so much time with her the evening before, but it was unrealistic to think he'd want to do it again. He had his own life.

A life without his best friend's little sister demanding his attention.

"One night." She lifted her index finger to emphasis her point. "By then, this whole unfortunate incident will be behind us. I'm sure of it."

Jude beamed. "Great! Do you want me to pick you up after work? Then we can make a run through the market for junk food and whatever else tickles our fancy."

"Sure. I'll be at the food pantry all day so you can swing by around 6:00."

Jude stood, her smile still stretching her mouth from ear to ear. "See you then."

Folding her arms on the desk, she lowered her head and sighed. All her life she'd battled the stereotype of being the helpless baby sister, and here she was, everyone's charity case again.

But she wasn't helpless. Wasn't someone to be pitied or treated like a fragile piece of glass. She'd survived more violence and trauma than most people would ever know, and she'd survive this too. Maybe she should shift her perspective. Look at this as an opportunity to mend old wounds and find peace for once in her life. That was really the only way to move forward.

"Laura?"

Cade's booming voice popped up her head and sent her heart into a gallop. He stood in front of her with his laptop bag over his shoulder and an armload of files.

She smiled, picturing Cade looking the exact same way the night before. "Déjà vu."

"Huh?" His dark eyebrows snapped together.

"Never mind. Ready to go?"

"Yeah. Still didn't find anything missing, so that's good and bad."

She shut down the laptop on her desk and gathered the power cords. "How so?"

"Good that nothing important was stolen, but bad because it makes it look like you were the target. Not the office."

"You're right. That is bad." A shudder ripped down her spine as she placed the computer and its accessories in her tote bag. She studied the desk for anything else she should take, and the flash drive she'd found the night before caught her eye. She grabbed it and tossed it in the bag.

"What's that?"

She shrugged. "Not sure. I found it in the desk last night but didn't get a chance to look at it. I'll let you know what's on it if anything important pops up. Probably an old flash drive someone threw in the drawer and forgot about. Ready?"

He stepped to the door and opened it wide. "After you."

Standing, she hooked her bag on her shoulder and hurried outside. The bright sun urged her forward, and she picked up her pace, chin lifted.

Yes, shifting her perspective was exactly what she needed.

She was strong. She was fierce. She was a survivor. And come hell or high water, she'd pave the way for a bright future for her and child. And God help the man who tried to stop her.

6

B oxes of fresh fruits and vegetables, stacked in the entryway of the food pantry, greeted Laura. She stepped around them, spinning in a circle to take in the produce. "What is all this doing here?"

"No clue." Cade set his computer bag on a wooden bench built into the wall. The dark wood matched the curving staircase that led to the second and third floors. "But it's a weird place to store food."

A door on the opposite side of the foyer swung open. Mrs. Collins strode in, a smile on her lips and whistle chirping from her mouth. "Ah, good morning, you two. Do you mind giving me a hand?"

"Sure," Laura said, placing her belongings next to Cade's. "Whatever you need."

"Don't make promises you can't keep because I won't forget them." Mrs. Collins winked then chuckled. "But for now, if you could help me carry all these boxes into the kitchen, I'd be eternally grateful."

"Not a problem." Laura scooped up a box filled with leafy greens and followed Mrs. Collins into the kitchen.

Light spilled through the lone window above the sink. But even the golden beams couldn't chase the gloom from the small space. The limited counters were cluttered with boxes and canned foods, so Laura placed her cargo on a rectangular island on wheels in the middle of the room. "Is there enough space in here to fit everything?"

"Absolutely not. That's what he's for." Mrs. Collins tilted her head in Cade's direction. "I need a bigger kitchen to accomplish all the things simmering around in this head of mine."

Cade set his stash of apples on the ground then turned around to grab more.

Intrigued, Laura leaned against the counter. "What do you have planned?"

Mrs. Collins blew out an exaggerated breath that pushed her bangs up in the air. "For starters, I'd love a bigger refrigerator to fit all these donations, but that's just the tip of the iceberg. I need more counter space, more storage, more cabinets. I want to open the pantry up for more than merely a place to grab some canned goods. I want to make this a community. A place for a free meal or a table to sit at with peers. I want a sanctuary. A haven for everyone who needs it."

The idea took hold of Laura with such force, tears gathered at the corners of her eyes. She'd needed a lifeline like Mrs. Collins described so many times. Needed a community to offer support and encouragement—to let her know she wasn't alone.

Even now that she'd left Isaac and struck out on her own, she struggled to keep putting one foot in front of the other. Struggled to earn enough money to pay for both rent and a meal. And that was with having people lending a hand or offering her a way to help herself. There had to be so many other people out there in similar situations who needed exactly what Mrs. Collins described.

"Oh, honey. What's wrong?" Mrs. Collins engulfed her in a hug and held her close.

Laura held on tight, soaking up all the warmth the older woman offered. "Nothing. Everything. I don't know."

"You just let it all out."

She sniffed back her tears and pulled herself together. "What you said was so beautiful. You want to give back to people you don't even know. What you're providing—what you plan to provide—is such a huge gift."

Mrs. Collins tucked her thumb under Laura's chin and stared into her eyes. "That's the best thing about gifts. We all have them, and we can all give them. Which is why I now have a surplus of produce that'll probably go bad before I can give it away."

The door swung open again, and Cade backed into the kitchen balancing three more boxes.

"Maybe we can figure out how to get the food out to the community before it spoils," Laura said. She eyed the produce, inwardly cringing at throwing away any food.

"How do you propose we do that?" Mrs. Collins fisted a hand on her hip. "I hate the stigma surrounding the people who come here for help. In small town like this, perception is everything. Some people don't want to be gossiped about or are concerned with what others might think if they seek help."

Now Laura cringed on the outside. That's why she hadn't been to the food pantry even though her cabinets were often bare, and she'd gone to bed more than one night hungry. "Then we make something delicious with this food and we take it out into the community. We spend the day spreading your kindness and your vision then hope they take root and grow until this place is bursting with more than donations."

Mrs. Collins clapped her hands like an excited child. "I love that idea."

Laura glanced at Cade's frown and winced. "Is that okay? Sorry, I know I'm working for you today."

He shrugged, his mouth hitching up on one side. "We

wanted to ask Mrs. Collins if you could work here instead of the office. What you do while you're here is up to you. Besides, I don't have much for you today anyway. And you can get a better idea of how we can improve the kitchen if you're working in it."

"Wait," Mrs. Collins said. "I'm thrilled to have you, but why don't you want to work from the office?"

"There was a break-in last night. I'm a little uneasy about spending the day there."

"Then you'll stay right here with me as long as you need." Mrs. Collins draped an arm over her shoulder and pulled her close.

Warmth spread through her at the pure sincerity pouring from Mrs. Collins, but she needed to make sure the other woman understood she might be putting herself in the line of fire. "Are you sure? I don't want to bring danger to your doorstep."

A hard glint sparked in Mrs. Collins' gray eyes. "Bring it on. I'm tougher than I look and would kill to protect those I care about."

The ferocity of her words calmed Laura's anxiousness. Mrs. Collins might be pushing seventy, but Laura didn't doubt she was a tough bird. Someone who would do whatever it took to stand for those who needed her.

Someone with a past that must have turned her into the woman she was today.

"Do you have a place I can set up my computer?" Laura asked. "I promise to stay out of the way."

Mrs. Collins hooked her arm in Laura's. "I have just the place. We'll get you situated then I'll be the one bothering you. First in the kitchen, then out on the town to spread the news about the new vision for the pantry along with a delicious treat."

"We appreciate your hospitality, but I'm not sure if being

out alone is a good idea," Cade said. "Might be better to stay inside until we have more answers."

"She'll be with me. In daylight around plenty of people. No one will hurt her."

Laura couldn't hide her smile at Mrs. Collins' confidence and held Cade's gaze for a beat.

His eyes widened then he a gave a brief nod. "Please be careful and let me know where you are if you don't mind. I'll get to work."

Laura let Mrs. Collins lead her out of the kitchen. She may have found a new friend in the most unlikely of places.

SAVORY SCENTS WAFTED up the stairs to the library where Cade had been working for hours. He'd kill to have a room like this in his house. Floor to ceiling bookshelves covered one wall, filled with tomes of every color. The walls were a deep blue and two leather chairs sat in front of an ornate, marble fireplace. A generous bay window overlooked the back yard, which was overgrown and filled with weeds, a worn white fence enclosing it.

He'd spent the day drawing up plans and scheduling workers. As long as Mrs. Collins made quick decisions over the next couple days, and the supplies he needed weren't on backorder, work should begin in a week.

His stomach growled as he clicked out of the browser window on his computer. He'd done as much as he could for now. Almost time to break for lunch. Maybe sneak down to the kitchen and discover what Laura and Mrs. Collins had spent all morning making.

The workspace Laura had set up on a side table by the tufted sofa caught his attention. She'd placed the flash drive she'd mentioned in the computer but hadn't opened it.

Intrigued, he crossed the room to the worn couch and settled the laptop on his lap. He opened the imported file, and a spreadsheet filled with numbers took over the screen.

Great. More numbers.

He scrolled down in search of any clue as to what the numbers meant or alluded to, but nothing.

Buzz, buzz, buzz

He scooped his phone from his pocket and swore under his breath at Matthew's name on the screen.

"Where the hell have you been?" Unable to control his anger, he barked into the phone.

"Is Laura okay? Did they find the asshole who hurt her?"

"Yes, she's okay. No, they haven't found who broke in and hurt her. No thanks to you on either count."

A low grumble sounded through the phone. "I've had shit on my plate."

"Really? Because I don't remember you telling me about anything you have going on. Just you cutting and running with no explanation then not answering your damn phone when we needed you."

"Well, I'm back now," Matthew snapped. "Standing in the office and no one is here."

"Didn't know I needed to punch a freaking card." Cade's irritation diffused a little knowing his friend and business partner was back in town. "Laura and I are at the food pantry. She didn't want to work in the office, and I didn't feel right leaving her alone. Someone came after her, and you weren't around when she needed you."

Matthew blew out a long breath. "I hate that I wasn't here, but like I said, I've been dealing with my own shit. Thanks for looking after her. I tried calling her before you, but she didn't answer. I need to tie up some loose ends then I'll touch base with her tonight."

"Before you go, quick question."

"What?"

Exhaustion made the word sound heavy, causing tingles of alarm to ripple through Cade. Matthew was always the happy one. The friendly one. The one most clients dealt with because of his quick wit and ever-present smile. Something was off, but Cade wouldn't push. Not when he hated people to press into his business when all he wanted was to shut the world off for a while and process things.

He'd give Matthew some space. Respect his way of dealing with whatever was going on but be prepared to swoop in and help Matthew with his shit.

Until then, he still needed his partner to help run their company.

"Laura found a flash drive in the desk in the reception area. I just opened the files that are on it, and I can't figure out what the hell it means. It's a spreadsheet with a bunch of numbers. No notes or explanations. Any idea what it's from?"

Matthew snorted. "I told you to leave the numbers to Laura."

"Shut up, dipshit, and answer the question." He rolled his eyes. Numbers might not be his favorite thing to stare at, but he wasn't an idiot.

"Don't have a clue what it is. I don't think I've ever sat at that desk. Honestly, never understood why we even had it."

"Because we planned to hire a secretary." Pain pulsed at this temple, and he set the computer aside.

"That's right. We've always just shoved unwanted crap in there. I'm sure it's some random flash drive we didn't want anymore. No need to waste your time on it. I gotta run. I'll lock up the office and head out, but we'll get together soon."

The call disconnected before Cade could get in another word. He tossed the phone beside him and leaned his head back to stare up. A dusty chandelier hung from the center of the room and wood beams created squares across the ceiling.

A soft knock sounded. "Am I interrupting something?" Laura asked with an airy laugh. "Some deep thinking perhaps?"

The lightness in her voice lifted his lips. "Just pondering life's biggest questions. Like what's on the flash drive you found and what did you make downstairs that smells so amazing."

"I can answer one of those questions easily. You're smelling freshly baked apple pies and banana bread. The second one I'd need to take a look at the files." She rounded the corner of the couch and picked up the computer before sitting. "Is it on here still?" she asked, tilting her head toward the now-open screen.

He scooted closer and the urge to brush a dusting of flour off the exposed column of her neck made his blood boil.

Narrowing her eyes, she studied the screen. "Mostly two rows. All numbers. Interesting how the rows on the left all have larger numbers than the ones on the right."

She pecked at the keys and input some formula that went right over his head into the spreadsheet.

"What are you doing?"

"Just curious. I want to know what happens if you add these numbers together or subtract one from the other." She highlighted numbers then input more.

Okay. Matthew had been right. Laura was much smarter than he'd realized.

"Interesting," she said.

"What do you see?"

"Yesterday I spent a lot of time studying the finances. I wanted to get familiar with everything in the office." She spared him a quick look. "Hope I didn't overstep."

He shook his head. "Not at all."

"These numbers here." She trailed the pad of her pinky down the row, showcasing the new numbers that had appeared after she'd put in one of her formulas. "They look familiar."

More pecking at the keys. More spreadsheets popped up on the screen. "See. Same numbers."

"And those numbers are?"

"These show the amount paid for past projects."

He furrowed his brow, trying to keep up. "And how did you make the numbers from the flash drive match the ones in our accounting books?"

"I subtracted one from the other. Not all of your projects are listed on the drive. But enough that the patterns are clear. It's not a coincidence."

That made him sit straight. "No. Not a coincidence. But something definitely isn't adding up."

7

Laura studied the numbers again, willing everything to make sense. The heat of Cade's gaze on her face made her squirm, but no matter how much she spun it, things didn't add up.

More accurately, they added up in a way that told an alarming story.

"This is bullshit." Cade jumped to his feet and paced across the room in front of her.

"Perhaps. Maybe there's more to the picture than I'm seeing. I mean, I don't know much about business. Especially yours. Matthew would be a better person to look at this than me."

Cade shook his head. "I just talked to him. Asked him about the flash drive and he didn't know anything about it. Which means he wouldn't understand what's on there anymore than us, or he's lying."

"You don't really think he'd lie, do you?"

He threw up his arms. "I don't know what to think right now. Matthew's always been the money guy. He handles our accounts, books the clients, discusses payments. When I try to get a better handle of things, he shoos me away and tells me not to worry about it. Even with only being gone one damn night he brought you in. Asked you to help out. For what? It doesn't make sense."

She bristled at his irritation. She hadn't questioned Matthew asking her to step in. Hell, she'd looked at it as an opportunity to create a better situation for herself and her child. Cade acted as if the idea of her working for the construction company was one he found absolutely appalling. Yet another example of his best friend's little sister pushing in and being a nuisance.

"Maybe he wanted to help his sister," she snapped. "Give me a job where I'm not on my feet all damn day as my belly and ankles get bigger. Let me use my brain for once. Give me a chance to do more. To be more."

Cade stopped and turned toward her, eyes wide. "I didn't mean anything. I'm sorry. I'm just confused and anxious and a little pissed."

She blew out a long breath and steadied her nerves. "It's fine. But there has to be a logical explanation. Call Matthew again and let him know what we found on the flash drive. He might have different insight to help us get to the bottom of things."

"No." He squeezed the bridge of his nose. "Not yet."

She lowered the computer beside her, alarm tightening her core. "Why not? He's your best friend and partner. He's my brother. He deserves to know if we suspect something's going on with the business."

"And he will. Once we figure out exactly what is going on. Or at least have a better understanding of everything. But I need a chance to wrap my head around this. Time to look at things for myself."

Something about the tight set of his broad shoulders, the ticking of the vein by his temple, made her uneasy. "Do you think Matthew has something to do with this?"

The question seemed to deflate him. He made his way back to the couch and sunk down beside her. "I don't want to think so, but...." He trailed off as if unable to even finish the thought.

No. She couldn't sit and listen to this. Matthew was a good man. The only person who'd always shown her love and compassion. "There has to be another answer. Who all has access to your accounts? To your office?"

He let his head fall back, returning to the same position he'd been in when she'd entered the library. "Me and Matthew."

She bit her bottom lip. "Who talks to the accountant?"

"Matthew."

"Collects payments? Makes the budget? Submits bids?"

"Matthew, Matthew, Matthew."

"Well, hell." She let her head fall back like his.

He turned to face her. "Will you help me figure out this mess? You're brilliant, way smarter than me. Not to mention you have some distance, a different viewpoint."

"You think I'm brilliant?" She shifted and stared directly into his eyes.

"I do. And more importantly, I trust you."

His admission untied some of the knots in her gut. "Okay then. I'll help you. But you have to promise we'll tell Matthew everything soon. I don't want to keep secrets from him."

"Deal."

"Where do we start?"

He fell forward, bracing his elbows on his knees. "I don't know. My head is spinning. None of this makes sense."

Wanting to offer him the same amount of comfort he had her, she rested a hand on his bicep. "We'll figure it out. I promise. There has to be a reasonable explanation right under our nose. We just don't see it yet."

He sighed, not looking convinced. "I hope you're right."

Her brain spun in circles as she tried to figure out the best way to tackle the problem.

"There you are," Mrs. Collins said in a sing-song voice. "I thought you were coming right back. I've got everything packed and ready to go. If we leave now, things will still be nice and warm upon delivery."

Laura cringed. Crap. She'd forgotten about assisting Mrs. Collins with the baked goods. "I'm so sorry. Some things have come up unexpectedly."

Cade sat straight and bumped her knee with his. "You should go. You were excited about it this morning. I need time to wrap my mind around this. I'm going to head back to the office and start pouring through files. By the time you're down, maybe I'll have a better plan."

She frowned, torn between the commitment she'd made to Mrs. Collins and sticking around for Cade.

As if reading her mind, he placed a hand on hers and tingles of excitement shot up her arm. "Really. Go. I need a second to absorb everything."

"Okay. We won't be gone long."

She offered him a smile then hurried to the kitchen, Mrs. Collins behind her. The sooner they started the sooner they'd finish, and she could get back to helping Cade.

"Is everything all right?" Mrs. Collins hooked the handle of a giant basket in her arm before handing another her way.

Laura blew out a shaky breath. "I hope so."

Ignoring the sinking feeling in the pit of her stomach, she grabbed the rest of the goodies she and Mrs. Collins had prepared and headed out the door that led to the backyard. The grass was overgrown, and weeds had taken over a small patch of land intended for a garden. Wildflowers mingled with dandelions along the back of the house.

Mrs. Collins sighed. "So much to do in this place, so little time."

Laura glanced around the fenced-in area before following through the gate to the sidewalk. "Have you owned the home long?"

"It's been in my family for decades. I gained ownership when my older sister passed away. The house had been too much for her to manage, and she never would accept help, so a lot has fallen into disarray."

"When did you start the food pantry?" Laura asked, stepping beside her. She'd lived in Pine Valley her whole life and hadn't given much thought to the food pantry or what it provided the community. She'd been too busy surviving and wasn't aware of something she didn't need at the time.

"Not too long ago. I started small. Setting out a stand by the road with a sign and food to give away. Then inviting people who returned inside to go through the pantry. When word spread, people started dropping off donations. Now I put up flyers around town. Do what I can without spending too much money. But I want to see more growth. Figure out how to help more people."

Now Laura was happy she'd taken the time to help Mrs. Collins with her mission. Cade might need her, but this was important, and she was happy to do something for someone else for a change.

They turned the corner and headed toward the middle of town. A few pedestrians strolled along the well-kept sidewalks, pushing strollers or walking hand-in-hand with little ones. It wouldn't be long before she had her own baby to push through the quiet streets. The thought warmed her more than the bright sun overhead.

"Where should we start?" Mrs. Collins asked.

Laura stopped and studied the storefronts. Colorful awnings were pulled over glass windows. A few tables lingered in the shade, providing seating in front of the bakery and a new café she hadn't tried yet. Buckets of colorful flowers showed off the florist's works without having to step into her shop.

A thrift store caught her eye. "What about Sweet Repeats? Looks like there's quite a few people inside, and I'd feel weird bringing food to one of the restaurants."

Mrs. Collins chuckled. "Agreed."

Laura led the way to the store. She opened the door and a little bell chimed, announcing their arrival. Racks of clothes and restored furniture welcomed them. Every inch of space was covered with something beautiful, and Laura had to stop herself from riffling through the baby cloths she'd spied.

A woman with bright hazel eyes and a brighter smile approached them. Her strawberry blond hair curled around her face. "Hello. Can I help you find anything?"

Mrs. Collins grinned. "Oh, I think I could get lost finding all sorts of fun things in here, but that'll have to wait for another time."

The woman raised an amused brow. "Ok. What can I do for you today?"

"Well, I'm Mrs. Collins and this is Laura. We come bearing treats—freshly baked from the food pantry I run."

"How lovely. I'm Elsie, by the way, and this is my store. That's so kind of you to stop and offer something yummy for me and my customers. I'm fairly new in town. I didn't realize there was a food pantry."

"Sadly, a lot of people don't," Laura said, knowing that was only partially true. Some folks, like her, knew it was there but were afraid to be seen using such an amazing resource. "We're trying to fix that. One piece of apple pie at a time."

Elsie's eyes widened. "I'd love to help spread the word. Do you have a flyer or something I could hang up?"

Mrs. Collins pulled a folded piece of paper from her pocket. "I always come prepared."

While Mrs. Collins handed over the flyer, Laura placed a

few more pieces of pie on the glass counter for customers then wandered through the racks of clothes. "You have super cute stuff."

"Thanks," Elsie said, beaming. "I love taking something used and discarded and turning it into something beautiful. Something that will make someone else happy. Be treasured."

Laura let the sentiment sink in while glancing at the cutest onesies. She'd been afraid for so long to tell Isaac about her pregnancy, that she'd gone through the last six months in some weird haze. Almost as if she didn't tell him, then she wasn't really carrying his child. As excited as she was to be a mom, she was terrified. Terrified of raising a baby all on her own, and even more terrified of keeping her baby safe from the man who helped create it.

"Boy or girl?"

She glanced over her shoulder and found a tall woman with a lovely face covered in freckles standing close. A young girl around the age of five stood beside her, holding her hand. "I don't know."

"Are you waiting to be surprised?"

She shrugged. "I don't really have a plan. For anything."

"Nobody does. Hold on a second." The woman disappeared behind another rack of clothes and came back with a gray, short-sleeved onesie with the words *Mama's Sweetie* scrawled across the material in big, bold letters. "Here. Perfect for a boy or a girl."

A rush of emotions tightened Laura's chest. She gently took the little piece of clothing and ran her fingertips down the front. As much as she wanted to purchase the item, the small number in her bank account flashed in her mind.

"Mommy, I want pie." The little girl pulled on the woman's hand.

"One second my love." She smiled at Laura. "Sorry, I didn't

mean to intrude. I'm Sadie. And this impatient child who smells pie is Amelia."

She smiled down at the little girl. "Nice to mee you, Amelia. That pie was made fresh and with lots of love."

"Did you bake it?" Sadie asked.

She refocused on the other woman. "Yes. I came in with Mrs. Collins to spread the word about the food pantry."

Interest brightened Sadie's green eyes. "A food pantry? Do you need volunteers?"

Laura bit into her lower lip and tried to capture Mrs. Collins' attention. "You'd have to ask her, but I'm sure she'd love the help. She has grand plans."

"I'll do that. Thanks."

Amelia hopped up on her tip toes and waved a teddy bear in the air. "Mommy's buying me this. I love stuffies."

As if spurred on by the little girl's sweet voice, a gentle kick fluttered inside Laura's stomach. She sucked in a breath and cradled her bump with her hand.

"Are you okay?" Sadie asked.

She chuckled. "Yes. The baby kicked."

"She must love stuffies, too," Amelia said with so much confidence Laura believed her. "Or me. Can I buy the baby that shirt? We can be friends."

"Oh, no. That's very sweet but not necessary."

Sadie rolled her eyes and held out a palm. "Now that it's in her head, she won't rest until her mission's complete. You'd be doing me a huge favor if you let me get that for you."

Laura hesitated.

"Pretty please?" Amelia asked.

The pleading combined with the jutted out bottom lip was Laura's undoing. "I'll make you a deal. I'll let you buy it for my baby if you eat the biggest piece of pie on the counter."

Amelia's smile grew wider, showcasing a missing front tooth. "Deal!"

Sadie laughed. "Twist her arm. I'll ask about volunteering as well. Maybe we'll see you around."

"I hope so," Laura said, walking with them to the front of the store.

Once Sadie had paid for her wares, she handed Laura the bag and led Amelia out of the store. Gratitude curled her toes. She'd started her mission with Mrs. Collins to help her and ended up gaining so much.

Cade's story from earlier in the day came back to her. When he'd been in a dark place, he'd used what he loved to bring himself into the light. Maybe that's what she needed to do. Use her gifts or talents or her passion to find her way forward.

With a lightness in her step she hadn't felt in years, she stepped out of Sweet Repeats and into the bright sunshine.

And right into Isaac.

8

Cade poured over file after file on his computer, comparing what he found to the paper receipts and statements kept in the cabinet in the reception area. Everything added up. Everything made sense.

But a sinking feeling in his gut told him he was missing something. Something really freaking important.

Crinkled papers and empty manilla folders cluttered his desk. He hung his head in his hands. The only place left to search was Matthew's office. The idea of rifling through his best friend's personal belongings—related to their business or not—didn't sit well with him. Even if it was something that had to be done.

A soft knock at his door shot up his aching head.

Deputy Owen Wells stood in the doorway and lifted a hand in greeting. "Evening."

Cade rose to his feet and crossed the room, offering his palm to the sheriff's deputy. "Do you have any news about the break-in, Deputy?"

"Please, call me Owen," he said, accepting the handshake before dropping his arm to his side. "Sorry, but no. I was stopping by on my way home. Just wanted to check to see how you and Ms. Metcalf are doing."

Cade shoved a hand through his hair and glanced back at the mess on his desk. "I've been better."

"Sorry to hear that. Is there anything I should know about? Anything I can help with?"

Cade debated spilling his twisted guts to the deputy, but what good would it do? Right now, all he had was speculation and intuition. He had no concrete proof that anything fishy was going on besides the numbers on the flash drive.

But who put the flash drive in the desk to begin with?

"Mr. Sulley?"

Cade blinked back to the present and tried to quiet the voices in his head. "Sorry. What?"

"Has anything else happened I should be aware of?"

He blew out a long breath. "Isaac Heck showed up at Laura's this morning. He was pissed someone asked him for an alibi."

"Dammit. I was afraid that might happen. I went to his house myself because I wanted to get a good read on him. I could tell he was struggling to keep his composure. Is he a threat to Laura?"

Cade snorted. "I'm surprised you even have to ask. People around town all seem to know their history."

One dark brow rose high on Owen's face. "The sheriff's department doesn't do much in these parts. The local force usually has a handle on things. The only reason I stepped in to assist on the break-in was because your office is technically out of the city limits."

Debating how much to divulge, Cade scrubbed a palm over his face. Spikes of scruff scaped over his skin, reminding him he hadn't had a chance to shave. He wasn't in the habit of spreading around people's personal business, but Laura was in danger.

And Isaac's treatment of Laura over the past few years wasn't exactly a secret.

"Isaac is bad news. Always has been. Even as a kid, he was trouble. Mean as snake, sneaky, and manipulative."

"Is there a history of violence between him and Ms. Metcalf?"

The question made Cade's blood boil. "You could say that. He's left bruises all over her for years. She finally left him a few months ago, and I think everyone who knows her is holding their breath, waiting for him to strike. Especially with the baby on the way."

Owen worked his jaw back and forth. "And the local police never did anything about this?"

"Laura never pressed charges. Not really sure why. Honestly, I'm still shocked she left. And now she's facing the same old shit. Looking over her shoulder and fearful of being attacked."

"I'll make sure to stick as close to town as I can. Keep an eye on the guy. His alibi holds, but that doesn't mean he doesn't play a role in this. Anything else I should know about him?"

"If he sees you around, he'll try and be your pal. Try to show you he's not a threat. He knows when to turn on the charm. Hell, even Laura's own father has a soft spot for the asshole."

Owen crossed his arms and furrowed his brow. "Really?"

"Isaac works for Mayor Metcalf. Likes to rub it in everyone's face he has an in with such a high-profile figure in the community."

Red flashed across Owen's face and highlighted his chiseled jaw. "If I had a daughter, I'd do whatever I could to keep her safe and away from someone hurting her."

"Agreed." The sentiment clenched his stomach muscles. Laura had put her relationship with Isaac behind her, but he was still the father of her child. How could she keep him from getting his hands on the innocent baby?

A flash of protectiveness swept through him—a sudden urge to see Laura and make sure she was safe tightening his muscles. He glanced at his watch and frowned. He'd been in the office for over an hour. Laura and Mrs. Collins should be finished passing out their treats.

"Somewhere you need to be?" Owen asked.

"Kind of," Cade said, scratching his chin. "Laura should be here by now. Let me call and find out where she is. Can you give me a minute?"

"Yeah, sure. No problem."

Cade circled back to his desk and grabbed his phone then called Laura. The line rang in his ear, increasing an impending sense of dread, until it went to voicemail. He disconnected and threw it on the desk. "Shit."

"Problem?"

"She didn't answer. With everything that's going on, I don't like the thought of her walking around town alone. Something seems off."

"Then let's go." Owen reached into his pocket and pulled out his keys.

"Excuse me?"

"Well, if we need to find her, it'll be easier with two of us. I'll drive."

Not needing any more encouragement, he shoved what he needed in his pocket and followed Owen outside. He was probably overreacting. Laura and Mrs. Collins had probably gotten caught up chatting and lost track of time.

But a nagging feeling in his gut told him Laura was in trouble and he couldn't get to her fast enough.

～

Fear fisted Laura's throat. She tightened her grip on the shopping bag and glanced around. The sidewalks were empty. No traffic chugged along the quiet streets.

"Doing a little shopping?" Isaac took a step forward, pushing into her personal space.

She stepped back. Needing as much distance from him as she could get. "What are you doing here? Are you following me?"

He laughed, the sound raising the hairs on her arms. "Seriously? Don't you think I have more important things to do?"

She knew better than to answer the question. No matter what she said he'd find a way to twist her words. To make it sound like she was the crazy one.

"Since you're too selfish to ask, I'll go ahead and tell you what I was doing. I was at the bakery and spied you walking over to this cheap shop. Thought I'd come over and say hello. We have a lot to figure out." He dropped his gaze to her stomach and smiled.

She crossed her bump with her arms. "There's nothing to figure out. We have nothing to talk about. I just want you to stay away from me."

He pressed in closer, pinning her against the side of the building. "Not a chance in hell. I've let you make your point— throw a little tantrum and run away like a little brat. But enough is enough. Come home and we can start preparing for our baby."

"I already told you. You will never be near my child."

A familiar snarl twisted Isaac's mouth. He shot out his hand and gripped the back of her neck, putting his face inches from hers. "You'll never be rid of me. I have rights. I will enforce them. And if you make this difficult, I will ruin you."

She winced at the pain as he squeezed harder. Laura balled up her hand and knocked on the glass behind her, praying someone inside would see and come to her rescue.

"What the hell are you doi—"

The door swung open, the bell chiming, and cut off the rest of Isaac's words. "Can I help you with something?" Elsie stood in the doorway wielding a broom in her hand like a weapon. "I'm not sure my store has anything you'd be interested in, but I'd be more than happy to tell you where you can go."

Isaac loosened his grip on Laura's neck, looping his arm to hook around her shoulders. He tried to pull her to his side, but she refused to be moved.

He smiled, the devil inside him clear in his eyes. "We're just having a friendly chat. No need to concern yourself."

"There's nothing friendly about you or this conversation," Laura said, gaining confidence with Elsie's presence. "You need to leave. Now."

Isaac glared but put a little distance between them. "This isn't over."

A shiver raced down her spine, but she stood her ground.

Elsie took her hand and squeezed. "It's over for now."

"See you around." Isaac grinned and turned to walk away.

Laura let out a long, shaky breath. Her legs threatened to buckle, and her heartrate refused to slow. "Thank you."

"Do you want to come inside and sit? You're a little pale."

All she really wanted was to go home, crawl in bed, and forget she was forever tied to such a horrible man. How could she protect her child when she trembled in fear every time she saw Isaac? How could she protect herself?

"Honey," Elsie said, breaking into her thoughts. "You'll figure it out. I promise."

"How do you know?" She hated the pleading in her voice, but at the moment, helplessness weighed her down.

A whisper of a smile lifted the corners of Elsie's mouth. "Because you have to. Sometimes we face challenges in life we never imaged. Challenges that knock us down so hard, we think we can never stand up. But we have to get back up.

Because someone else depends on us." She nodded toward Laura's stomach. "When the baby comes, you'll fight harder than you ever thought possible. Trust me."

She may have just met Elsie, but something in the way she spoke made Laura believe her. Made her want to know more about her and what had brought her to Pine Valley.

Before she could ask, a deputy cruiser pulled up to the curb. Cade's anxious face in the passenger window sent such a wave of relief crashing against her, threatening to steal her breath.

Cade jumped from the car and rushed toward her. "Are you all right? You look upset."

She forced a tight smile. "Just another lovely encounter with Isaac."

A low growl rumbled from Cade's chest.

The same deputy who'd talked with her after the break-in the night before jogged to them.

"Isaac was here," Cade muttered.

"Did he hurt you?" the deputy asked. "Threaten you?"

"Not any more than usual," she said with a small snort. "Snarky comments aimed at making me feel small."

Cade tightened his fist at his sides. "I shouldn't have left you."

"You can't be with me all the time. And I'm fine, really. Just shaken."

"Do you want me to give you a ride somewhere?" Deputy Wells asked.

"My sister is meeting me back at the food pantry soon. I can walk. Besides, I can't leave Mrs. Collins. She's still inside, talking with customers."

"If you want to leave now, I can grab her." Elsie gave her hand another squeeze then disappeared inside the store to fetch Mrs. Collins.

"You sure you don't want a ride?" Deputy Owens asked.

"I'll walk with her." Cade shifted to stand beside her.

Her core tingled at his nearness.

Deputy Owens touched the brim of his hat. "Call if you need anything at all."

She nodded and watched him get back in his vehicle and drive away, then faced Cade. The hard set of his jaw broadcast his anger. She hated that he was so affected by her mess. Needing to reassure him, she rested a hand on his arm.

The lines on his face relaxed and the corner of his mouth hitched up.

Butterflies erupted in her stomach. Holy hell, this man did things to her she never expected.

"I wish I'd been here when that little weasel popped up."

"You're here now, and that's all that matters."

Mrs. Collins stepped outside and frowned. "Are you okay?"

Laura stared up at Cade, their eyes locking, and nodded. "I will be."

And no matter how much Isaac terrorized, as long as Cade stood beside her, she knew it was true.

9

S tepping into the old Victorian house behind Laura, Cade's temper had finally cooled. He wished he could yell or scream or actually do something to keep Isaac away from Laura, but his hands were tied.

Worse yet, so were Laura's.

Mrs. Collins led the way into the cramped kitchen and put the baskets she'd hauled around town where they belonged. "I wish I'd been outside with you, Laura. I'd have given that young man a piece of my mind."

Laura sighed and plopped onto the stool in front of the mobile island. "I appreciate that, but there's nothing you could have done. Isaac will always find a way to barge into my life. I can't run away. I can't hide. I have to figure out how to live knowing he might be lurking around the corner."

Cade shook his head, his irritation climbing back up. "He shouldn't be allowed anywhere near you. He deserves to be in a jail cell."

"He'll get what's coming to him," Mrs. Collins said with a sympathetic smile. "People always do. But for now, I need to take advantage of the sunshine and get to work outside. Those weeds won't pull themselves."

"Would you like some help?" Cade asked, while silently hoping the answer was no. Gardening wasn't his thing, and no way he'd want Laura out in the hot sun after the day she'd had. But he also didn't want to leave her alone, even if she were mere feet away on the other side of a wall.

Mrs. Collins waved away his offer. "Nah. The garden is my happy place. You two stay inside. Help yourself to anything in the kitchen. Look around the house if you'd like. Maybe discuss all the wonderful ways you can transform this old place into exactly what I envision." She offered them a wink before heading outside.

Laura chuckled. "She's a firecracker."

"Hmm," he said, agreeing but unable to speak. He was too anxious, too worked up. His nerves demanded he move, do whatever he could to take care of Laura. An instinct that confused and scared the hell out of him. "Can I get you anything? Maybe some tea or something to snack on before Jude gets here?"

"Tea would be wonderful. I spied some in the cabinet to the left of the stove along with some mugs."

He went to work heating water and preparing tea. Silence fell between them, but there was nothing awkward or strained about it. Despite the stress surrounding them, Laura was easy to talk—or not talk—to. Easy to be around. Easy to love.

The thought made him flinch as he carried the mug of hot tea to her, spilling scalding liquid on his hand. Good. He deserved the pain. Deserved to be reminded Laura was off limits. Matthew would have his head if he found out the depth of his feelings for Laura, no matter how well intentioned.

Laura was forbidden fruit.

"Are you okay?" she asked, accepting the mug and setting it in front of her.

"Yeah, just distracted. I have all this nervous energy swirling around and I don't know what to do with it."

Wrapping her hands around the mug, she took a quick sip then swished her lips to the side. "How about we get out of our heads for a little bit?"

"How do you propose we do that?"

She shrugged. "We could take Mrs. Collins up on her offer. This house is beautiful, and I'd love to see more of it. I know you've got most of your plans made, but it wouldn't hurt to see if anything else could be done with this space."

He'd walked through the home multiple times, but there was no harm doing it again. Especially if he was with Laura. "All right. Where do you want to start?"

"Might as well head up to the third floor and work our way down."

He tilted his head to the side, searching her face for clues of where her thoughts were. "You think Mrs. Collins wants to use the third floor as part of the food pantry?"

A shy smile lifted her lips, and she glanced away as she stood and led him out of the kitchen. "Who knows what could be done with this place with a little imagination."

He wondered on her words as they walked from room to room, making sure to skip over Mrs. Collins' private quarters, which were more like a mini apartment with her small kitchenette, bathroom, and living space. Although he'd already seen it, he marveled again at the woodwork and original mahogany floors. Most of the bedrooms had been closed off, leaving old furniture covered in dusty sheets.

His fingers itched to polish and construct and create something beautiful from a space that had been neglected for too long. This house had amazing bones. All it would take was a nip here and a tuck there to turn it into something spectacular.

Taking the final step back down to the foyer, Laura sighed and ran her fingertips along the top of the banister. "I wish Mrs.

Collins' vision spanned further than the kitchen. This place has so much potential."

He crossed his arms over his chest and leaned against the wall. "What do you mean? She runs a food pantry. She wants more space for storing and preparing food. I agree this house is amazing, but there's no reason for further renovations based on her needs."

Laura nibbled her bottom lip and averted her gaze like a child with a secret.

"What is it?"

"What if this place could be more?" She finally met his eyes, and a light sparked in hers, bringing something to life inside her he'd never seen before.

He weighed his words carefully, not wanting to dim her excitement. "There's plenty of empty rooms that could be utilized, but Mrs. Collins never mentioned wanting anything other than some space on the first floor renovated."

"True, but she also—"

Two sharp knocks interrupted her thought moments before the door swung open. Jude and Brooke stood on the porch, each carrying plastic bags.

"Hope you don't mind Brooke joining us," Jude said, stepping inside and pressing a quick kiss to Laura's cheek.

"Before you answer that, I helped Jude talk Wade into making his famous fried chicken for us. We told him you'd asked for it." Brooke laughed and wiggled one of the bags in her hand.

Laura smiled. "The more the merrier."

Cade couldn't help the sigh of relief at seeing Brooke on the porch. It wasn't his job to tell Laura to be safe tonight or insist she let him sit in his car all night outside her house again. She wouldn't be alone with Jude, though he'd still worry. But Brooke was an ex-police officer who was more than capable of keeping Laura safe, and he had a sneaking suspicion that was the exact reason Jude had invited Brooke to their girls' night.

"Is there enough chicken for four?" he asked, his stomach growling at the smell of the meat wafting through the door.

Brooke grinned and pulled out a Styrofoam box. "Figured you'd ask."

He clasped a hand to his chest. "Bless you. I'll take this and get out of your hair." He took the offered meal then focused on Laura. "Call if you need anything. Anything at all."

She nodded.

The intensity of Jude and Brooke's gazes heated his skin, but he didn't care. All he cared about was making sure Laura understood he was there for her. No matter what.

Without another word, he walked out to his truck and headed toward home. Miles flew by, putting more and more distance between him and Laura. An ache burrowed into his chest.

Dammit. What was wrong with him? Laura was in good hands. Hell, he hadn't held a gun or stood guard since he'd left the Army. She was probably safer with Brooke anyway. He'd done nothing but disappoint and put others in danger when his job was to keep his men safe. He'd barely survived that. If something happened to Laura while she depended on him, he'd never get over it.

His tires crunched over loose gravel as he wove through the wooded lane toward his house. His big empty house where he'd eat alone, relax alone, and sleep alone. Parking the truck, he shoved a hand through his hair. He needed to get a grip. Stop obsessing over Laura and her safety and his feelings about her. He'd go crazy if he kept this up.

Decision made, he scooped up the bag from the passenger seat and stalked toward the front porch. He'd focus on his problems once he scarfed down the chicken and put Laura out of his mind for the night. He swung open the door, and fire shot through his veins.

The place was a mess. He took a step inside and dropped the bag. Cushions ripped from the living room sofa, pictures torn from the walls, glass shattered on the floor. He reached for his phone, fury shaking his hands, and unlocked the screen to call Owen. Someone hadn't simply broken into his home. They'd destroyed it. He flipped through his recent calls and found the deputy's number.

"Deputy Wells." Owen's voice came through the line, strong and steady.

"Hey, it's Cade. I—"

Thud!

A sudden flash of blinding pain slammed against the back of his head. His eyes fell shut and he crumbled to the ground as his consciousness flickered to oblivion.

LAURA'S ANKLES THROBBED. She propped them up on the coffee table while balancing a plate of half-eaten food on her stomach. She'd been starving when Jude handed her the full plate, but she couldn't eat another bite. Not with the baby squishing her organs and stealing her appetite.

"Do you need more water?" Jude asked. She sat cross-legged on the floor with her back against the recliner.

"I'm good, thanks. I'm so full."

Brooke set her empty plate on the coffee table then leaned back and rested her palms on her stomach. "Same. Will you judge me if I unsnap my jeans?"

Laura laughed. "I haven't snapped mine in months."

"You have an excuse," Brooke said. "I just like to eat."

Jude chuckled and stood, grabbing all the dirty dishes and carrying them to the kitchen. She returned with bags of Laura's favorite chocolates and tossed them on the sofa. "You sure you don't have any more room in there? I want my niece or nephew to come out all cute and chunky."

Groaning, she snatched up the bag and cracked it open. "You're killing me. You know I can't resist these."

"That's why I got them. I want to spoil you a little. Remember when we used to sit in our closet with a bag of candy and talk until all hours of the night?"

She smiled at the memory, even though Jude forgot to mention the reason they spent so much time in their closet was to hide from their dad. His moods swung from high to low like a pendulum, slamming against whoever was in his way.

Unwrapping a piece of milk chocolate, she popped it in her mouth and closed her eyes on a moan. "Spoil away."

"I'm glad you feel that way. I'd like to do more for you."

The tentative cadence of her sister's voice opened Laura's eyes. Her heart hammered against her breastbone. Rebuilding her relationship with Jude the last few months had taken a lot of work and faith that she wouldn't take off again. Having her sister back made it worth it, but she wasn't okay with being looked at like the tragic little sister who needed saving.

"What do you mean?"

Jude glanced over at Brooke then back to Laura. "Wade and I just bought a house, and we want you to move in with us."

Gratitude mixed with panic. "I appreciate the offer, I really do, but you and Wade are just starting your life together. You don't need me and a baby barging in and giving you responsibilities you didn't ask for."

"I want to help. I want to be here for you and for the baby. Being a single mother is going to be hard. I want to make up for lost time. To be your sister and the best aunt I can be. Wade's excited about it, too. I promise."

She hooked a brow, not buying that. "Really?"

Jude wrinkled her nose. "He will be when he sees the cute little baby."

Brooke laughed. "What about when that cute little baby is screaming all night?"

"It doesn't matter because it's not an option," Laura said. "This is my home. I'll figure this out, and you can come and visit any time you want. Trust me, I know I'll need help. But moving in with you and Wade is too much."

Jude kneeled in front of her and clutched her hands. "Can we try it? Just for a while. At least until whoever is after you is caught. I worry about you. Maybe not as much as Cade does, but I promise I do."

Heat slammed against Laura's cheeks. "He's only protective because it happened at his office. He's like another brother."

Brooke snorted. "I'm not sure about that."

The words made her pulse jump. "What do you mean?"

Brooke lifted a shoulder. "I could have peeled paint from a wall easier than Cade walking away from you today."

"Really? I've always thought he saw me as an annoying kid. He puts up with me because I'm Matthew's sister."

"Trust me, no man looking at you thinks you're just a kid. No matter who their friends are." Jude narrowed her gaze as if staring into Laura's soul. "You like him."

She squirmed under the scrutiny. "He's my friend."

"You *like* him," Jude screeched and slapped playfully at her arm. "Oh my God, Matthew's going to freak out."

"Oh, she's a grown-ass woman," Brooke said. "She doesn't need to worry about her brother's opinion."

"Whoa, hold on a minute." Laura lifted her palms, trying to keep up with the banter that had laid bare the feelings she thought she'd kept expertly hidden. "The last thing I need to be thinking about is Cade or anyone other than this little bundle in here. I have too much going on right now for my mind to even go to that place."

"That makes total sense," Brooke said, shooting Jude a pointed look that kept her quiet. "But I do agree with Jude on one thing. Being here alone isn't a great option while your assailant is out there."

All of her earlier ideas crashed back to her. She bit into her thumbnail, debating whether all the possibilities she'd imagined were fanciful dreams or a realistic goal. "You're right. Being pregnant and alone while some lunatic is out there isn't a great idea. But I'm not the only person in town with bad things happening. I'm not the only one who is scared and searching for a better future. A future that now seems harrowing and bleak."

"Oh honey." Jude squished between her and Brooke and hooked an arm around her shoulder.

"I'm not looking for pity," she cut in. "I'm just being realistic, while also realizing that as hard as it was to walk away from Isaac, I do have a support system. I have people in my corner who've stepped in. What about other women out there who don't have anyone?"

Brooke frowned. "The county has certain programs for those who need it. Then you have people like Mrs. Collins who are trying to help however they can."

"What if the food pantry could be more? I've spent some time with Mrs. Collins, and she's confided she wants her home to be a community, a haven, a safe place for those in need. What if we could do that by providing more than food?"

"Like what?" Jude asked.

"Like shelter and safety and a warm place to stay. There are so many empty rooms in that old house. We could make a women's shelter to help others get on their feet. Offer a helping hand to those who have no one in their lives to stand up for them." Excitement built in her chest as the words and ideas tumbled out of her mouth.

"That sounds amazing, but also like a lot of work. How could something like that work?" Jude asked.

"By taking it one step at a time," Brooke said, a smile growing wide. "When I got the idea to start Crossroads Mountain Retreat, I had no idea what I was doing. I just knew I wanted to make a difference. If I stepped back and looked at the big picture, I'd go straight to panic mode."

"So what did you do?" Laura asked.

"I made a plan then focused on the next step, then the next, then the next."

"Until you had it figured out?"

Brooke laughed. "I don't know if I have it figured out now. But the steps got easier, and the picture came more into view every day. All I know is your idea sounds amazing, and if it's something your gut is telling you to do, then figure out the next step."

"Are you sure you're up for something like this?" Jude asked.

Laura nodded. "I am. I need to focus on helping others. I need to do something positive. I think this could be life-changing for me and so many other women. I want to use the pain from my past to create something brighter and more beautiful."

Tears glimmered in Jude's eyes. "Then I'll do anything I can to help."

"Me, too," Brooke said. "So. What's the next step?"

Laura blew out a long breath. "Talking to Mrs. Collins. I want to make some notes, get my thoughts straight so she knows this is something I'm serious about. I don't want her to think I'm trying to take advantage of her."

She reached for her phone to jot down some ideas and the screen lit with an incoming call. An unknown number flashed on the screen. "Hello?"

"Ms. Metcalf, it's Deputy Owens."

Her breath caught in her throat. "Do you have news?"

"I do, but not the kind you want. Cade was attacked in his home tonight. He's at the hospital right now."

"Oh my God." She lifted a shaky hand to her mouth. Bile crept up her throat. Cade was hurt. "Thank you for letting me know."

She hung up and headed for the door. All thoughts except one leaving her head. She had to get to Cade.

10

The nurse in blue scrubs checked the machine monitoring Cade's vitals then tapped away on the tablet in her hands. The tight line of her mouth and narrowed eyes didn't give away a damn thing as he laid in the stupid hospital bed, waiting to be released.

"I hope that thing's telling you to let me leave." He tried to keep a lightness to his voice, but his words came out clipped.

The nurse offered him a small smile. "Sorry. I don't have that kind of power. But I can tell you everything looks good, and hopefully the doctor will be in shortly to spring you loose."

He mumbled a quick thanks then closed his eyes, wishing the bright florescent bulbs overhead could be dimmed. Anger continued to swirl inside him. Not only had someone invaded his sacred space and trashed it, but he'd been blindsided. Taken down without even catching a glimpse of the asshole who'd hit him.

"Cade?"

The sound of Laura's quiet, hesitant voice opened his eyes. He jolted up in bed and winced, bringing his fingers to touch the back of his head.

"Don't move." Laura hurried into the room, Jude and Brooke behind her.

A beat of excitement pushed down the nausea creeping up his esophagus, quickly replaced by embarrassment. As happy as he was to see Laura, this was the last place he wanted her to see him. Laid out on a hospital bed after being ambushed.

The thought was like a punch in the gut, bringing with it memories of another ambush. Another situation where he'd been caught off guard and others had paid the ultimate price.

Shoving those memories as far to the back of his mind as he could, he gritted his teeth and swung his legs over the edge of the bed.

Laura rested a hand on his shoulder, locking him in place. "Should you be moving? Are you all right?"

"I'm fine," he snapped, then cringed at his harsh tone when Laura's eyes widened. He blew out a long sigh to steady his nerves. "I'm sorry. I'm just tired and pissed and not feeling that great."

"We'll give you guys some space and wait in the lobby," Brooke said. "I'm glad you're okay, Cade. Is there anyone you want me to call?"

He pinched the bridge of his nose. Only the night before he'd sympathized with Laura when she'd been scared and hurting in the hospital, not wanting to call anyone to be with her. Now he understood her position. Alerting his family would only worry them.

Besides, the only person he wanted to see was already here.

"Nah. I can grab an Uber home or something. No need to alarm anyone."

Laura frowned, the V between her light brows deepening. "An Uber? Seriously? No way. We brought two vehicles. Brooke and Jude can drive back to my place—no need to stick around and wait—and I'll take you home."

"Are you sure?" Jude asked, taking a step inside the room. "We don't mind waiting."

Laura glanced over her shoulder and nodded. "I'm sure, as long as it's okay with Cade."

Cade forced a tight smile for Jude. "A ride home would be great."

"Okay," Jude said. "But both of you be safe or I'll stick to your sides like glue from now on. Call when you leave, please."

"Don't count on coming home to those chocolates. They're calling my name." Brooke hooked an arm around Jude's shoulders and led her out the door.

Laura waited for Brooke and Jude to leave then turned back toward him, worry shining bright in her blue eyes. "What happened?"

"When I got home, the place was a mess—broken into and wrecked. I grabbed my phone to call Deputy Wells and someone hit me on the back of the head. I woke to Deputy Wells and EMT's pulling into my driveway."

"Oh my God." Laura's hand went to the base of her throat. "Things could have been so much worse. Whoever was in your house could have killed you."

The crack in her voice squeezed his chest, and he pulled her to sit next to him. Her knee brushed against his, tightening his stomach muscles. "But they didn't. I'm okay. Just a little sore."

She wiped at her eyes. "Sorry. I know you're fine, but the thought of what could have happened is really scary. Or maybe it's just these stupid pregnancy hormones."

He captured her hand and squeezed, stopping her words. "Hey. Don't ever apologize for how you feel. Not around me. Besides, I might hate that this upset you, but it's nice to know you care."

"Of course I care," she said, her gaze locking on his.

A shudder stole his breath. What was he doing? He'd

fought his feelings for Laura for so long, but he was tired of it. Tired of telling himself she was off limits. Tired of telling himself staying away from her was better for them both. Tired of telling himself loving her was wrong.

A hammer of truth pounded against his already tender head. He loved Laura. Had for years. And dammit, if nothing else, the last couple days had shown him how much he wanted to have her in his life. And as much more than Matthew's little sister. No matter what his friend thought.

"Knock, knock. Mind if I step in?"

The same tall, slender doctor who'd examined Laura the night before waltzed into the room in blue scrubs and headed straight for the sink to wash her hands. Her long brown hair was pulled into a low ponytail. She turned to face them and smiled. "Can't say I'm happy to see you two in here again tonight, but I'm glad it appears your injuries are limited."

Laura made a move to stand, but he kept a firm grip on her hand, keeping her beside him. "We're about as happy to be here as you are to see us."

"I bet. In case you don't remember, I'm Dr. Simon." She crossed to the machine keeping track of Cade's vitals. "Things look good here. How are you feeling?"

"Pain meds are good, so not feeling too bad."

Dr. Simon let out a small laugh and shook her head. "Glad to hear it. Any nausea, dizziness, confusion?"

"Nope." Okay, so he might not be telling the exact truth, but no way he'd confess to anything that would keep him in the emergency room any longer than necessary.

"Well, since you lost consciousness for a few minutes, you do have a Grade II concussion. I need you to rest for the next couple of days. Take it easy. You can have over-the-counter pain medication for any discomfort, and it's best to have someone close by for the next twenty-four hours in case your symptoms worsen."

Laura rested her free hand on their joined ones. "I'll be there."

Her words hit him with the force of a knock-out punch, stealing his breath. Here was a woman who'd been through hell and was still fighting, even with the odds stacked against her. She wanted to be there for him. To stand with him and make sure *he* was okay.

Soaking up her support, he knew right then and there he'd do whatever it took to make sure Laura was safe. He'd be there for her any way she'd let him—to protect not only her but her child as well. Because deep in his heart, he knew he already loved them both.

LAURA JUMPED out of her car and rushed to help Cade. By the time she reached the front bumper, he'd already emerged from the vehicle. Moonlight filtered through the trees. His shoulders sagged and the normal scruff on his jaw had grown scraggly, giving him a harder edge than she was used to seeing.

An edge that somehow made him even sexier.

"Wait a second. Let me help you." He'd argued with the nurses about being wheeled out of the hospital when they'd left, but protocol didn't allow him to escape her pushing him from the emergency room to her car. Now she didn't have policies to help convince him to lean on her for support as she walked him to his front door.

"I'm fine," he said, although the tight line of his mouth told a different story.

She stayed glued to his side anyway, setting a palm on the middle of his back, as though that would do anything to steady him if a wave of dizziness hit. "I know you are, but the doctor gave me the task of making sure you stay fine, and I take that very seriously."

He snorted at her no-nonsense tone. "All I need right now is a hot shower and warm bed."

Images of Cade standing naked under a spray of water filtered into her head and she swallowed hard. Being in his home that morning had been torture as she'd heard the steady drum of water coming down, knowing he'd been just beyond the wall. So close her fingers itched to skim the coarse hair along his face and explore what lay below his well-fitting clothes.

She cleared her throat and ushered him up the porch steps. Man, these pregnancy hormones were messing with her in more ways than one. She needed to get a grip and fast.

Pushing open the front door and switching on the light, all thoughts of getting her hands on Cade evaporated. She gasped. He'd told her someone had broken in and trashed his home, but she'd been so worried about him she hadn't given much thought to the mess that awaited.

"Shit." Cade shoved a hand through his hair. "You should go home. Dealing with this mess is the last thing you should have to handle. I'll get to it later."

"I'm not going anywhere." She closed the door behind them and led Cade to the brown leather chair in his living room. Scanning the floor, she found the discarded cushion then returned it to its place before urging Cade to sit. "Can I get you anything?"

He shook his head then winced and pressed his fingers against his temples as he leaned back in the chair. "No thanks."

She let out a long breath. "Okay then. You sit and relax while I put this place back together."

"You don't have to do that."

"I know. I want to. You shouldn't have to do it alone."

She surveyed the destruction. Most of the damage didn't appear to be permanent. More like someone had come in and made the biggest mess they could manage. "Looks like a toddler came inside and threw a giant temper tantrum. Is the rest of the house like this?"

He shrugged. "I never got a chance to see. Deputy Wells assured me whoever had been here was gone by the time he arrived and encouraged me to report anything that was stolen. Other than that, your guess is as good as mine on how the other rooms look."

The touch of sadness in his voice cracked her heart in two. He'd opened up to her about how much his home meant to him. How building these walls had helped put him back together. Now someone had tainted his safe space. Had broken in and made this space ugly with their hatred and violence. She might not be able to help much, but she could bring the beauty back—the peace he'd found in this place.

"I can't tell if anything's been taken, but I can put things back where they belong. I'll make note of anything broken or damaged."

Without waiting for any more protests, she busied herself putting pictures back in their places—cleaning broken glass when necessary—and righted the furniture in the living room before tackling the kitchen.

She ran fingertips along the smooth marble island that separated the kitchen from the living room then gathered discarded dish towels and tossed utensils. She placed the cutlery and scattered dishes in the dishwasher and carried the soiled clothes to the laundry room down the hall. She flipped lights on as she entered each room. Every space in the house had been turned upside down. Every drawer dumped of its contents.

She stepped into the office and papers covered the floor like a blanket of makeshift snow. The filing cabinet was tipped on its side. A flash of gold caught her attention, and she rifled through the wreckage on the floor. A golden star looped in thick, blue ribbon lay amongst the heap, and she picked it up and studied the ornate medal.

Cade never spoke about his time in the military, but he'd clearly been given an award for something he'd done while in the line of duty. A lump lodged in her throat. His bravery and loyalty were constantly on display, probably why he'd been given this award, and it'd been cast aside like trash.

Actually, everything had been tossed aside like trash.

She straightened, gently placing the medal on the edge of the desk and hurried back out to the living room.

Cade was in the kitchen grabbing a glass from the cabinet. He glanced over his shoulder and offered her a weak smile. "You do quick work. Thank you."

She waved away his gratitude. "I've gone into every room, and they all look the same. Everything tossed around and a mess. I don't know what you own, but I have stumbled on some things that look valuable. Why wouldn't a burglar take them?"

Cade leaned against the counter and scratched his jaw. "That's a good question. The same thing happened at the office. Nothing was stolen, but we assumed that was because you were the target. Not anything at the office."

"What if I was just in the wrong place at the wrong time? What if someone came in after you left, not realizing they'd find anyone inside and panicked when they saw me just like they panicked when they saw you? What if I'm not the target at all?"

"That would mean they were after something and not someone," Cade said. "But what would I have here that anyone would go to all this trouble to get?"

She shrugged, mind spinning. "What's something they could have found at the office that might be here instead?"

He pinched the bridge of his nose, his energy deflated. "Who the hell knows? Files? Statements? But most of that is at the office or on my computer. I have project plans and some contract information here, but that's about it."

"What about that flash drive?" she asked, latching onto the idea. "Someone put it in the drawer. If we're right about what's on there, someone could want it back. Might want to make sure no one else gets their hands on it."

His gaze held hers, fire blazing in his eyes. "It's too late for that. But now we need to figure out what it means and fast before someone else gets hurt."

11

Exhaustion weighed down on Cade's shoulders. He practically melted against the supple couch cushions. The pounding in his head was more of an annoyance than anything—the over-the-counter medicine more than enough to take away the sharp edges of pain. His body yearned to fall into bed and sleep for the next twenty-four hours, but no way his mind would stop working long enough to actually rest.

Thanks to Laura, the house was mostly put back together. He'd called Deputy Wells and let him know not a single thing was missing. The deputy agreed—chances were high someone had broken in searching for something specific and he'd shown up at the wrong time.

Much like what happened to Laura.

But even though he could breathe a little easier knowing Laura wasn't the target, there were still too many unanswered questions for him to rest easy.

The back door from the deck slid open and Laura glided inside. "Mind if I join you?"

The only bright spot to all of the chaos was Laura, and damn was she one bright light. She'd worked tirelessly to help put his house back in order then forced him to eat something before taking a few minutes to herself to call her sister.

He could only imagine Jude's response to Laura staying at his place tonight. Probably better than what Matthew's would be, but he hadn't even called his best friend to fill him in on what had happened. He hated the sinking feeling in the pit of his stomach that told him something was off with Matthew, but he couldn't ignore it.

Ignoring his instincts had led to death and disaster in his past. He'd never make that mistake again.

Struggling to keep any strain from showing on his face, he straightened "Take a seat. Your feet must be killing you."

She shrugged and settled onto the opposite end of the couch. She shifted so her back pressed against the arm of the sofa, lifted her legs and leaned her knees against the back of the couch. Her feet were bare, toenails painted a siren's red. "My feet always seem to hurt these days, no matter what I'm doing."

He had to swallow the offer to rub them. His feelings for her might be clear as the crystal that had shattered in his kitchen, but he had to take things slow. Win her trust and let her know he was here for her and her baby.

Needing to think of something other than encasing the delicate arches of her feet in his hands, he changed the subject. "What did Jude say?"

Something flickered in her eyes, and she shifted her gaze to her clasped hands resting on her lap. "Not much. She's going to pack a bag and drop it off for me. Said she's glad you're feeling better."

"That's it?"

The corner of her mouth lifted slightly. "No, but that's all you need to hear."

He laughed, the sound grating against his sore head.

"Thanks for everything you've done. I appreciate it more than you know. "

"You would have done the same for me. Hell, you've done more than that the last couple days."

"All I've done is stick around."

"You've supported me, protected me, and helped spark an idea that could be life changing."

Intrigue moved him the tiniest bit closer to her. "How did I do that?"

She bit her bottom lip, as if unsure she should share.

Wanting to encourage her, he reached out and rested a hand on her knee. "Please. Tell me. I could use a distraction."

"I want to ask Mrs. Collins if we can turn the food pantry into a women's shelter." She blurted it out as if she'd been holding back the thought for days.

He absorbed her words, turning them around in his mind. "Was this why you wanted to take a closer look at the house earlier?"

She nibbled her thumbnail and nodded. "I want to get out of my head. Use my hands and my passion to create something beautiful. Just like you did with this place."

The softness of her voice made a lump grow in his throat. "I think that's a great idea. As long as Mrs. Collins agrees. It would be a lot of work for her. Much more than what she's taken on already."

"I could help, and there have to be more people in the community who would volunteer or use their skills to create something wonderful for women and children in need. If I can find a way to make it work, would you help with the construction? I'm sure the house wouldn't need much. There are plenty of rooms that only need a good scrubbing and some furniture. We could even transform some of the communal living spaces into specialty rooms to help with childcare or rooms for support groups. The possibilities are endless."

Her excitement made her come alive, and he had no trouble seeing her vision. The only issue was if Mrs. Collins would be willing to use her entire home for community outreach instead of the small section she currently utilized for the food pantry.

He didn't want to extinguish any of her enthusiasm, but he also wanted to make sure she understood how much she'd be asking of Mrs. Collins. "Your idea sounds amazing, and I'll help any way I can, but do you think Mrs. Collins would be on board to use her entire house for something like this?"

Uncertainty twisted her lips. "She's so passionate about providing a safe space for those in need. I hope she'll want to, but I don't want to place any pressure on her. I'll make sure she knows I can find another place for this. I mean, getting the funds for her remodel required some donations from the community. If that's what I have to do for a shelter, I will. I can feel it in my gut that this is something I need to see through. My past might be bumpy and filled with pain, but I have a support system to help. Not everyone's that lucky. I want to change that."

Pride swelled in his chest. "You will."

She beamed. "Thanks. Can you help me figure out how to approach Mrs. Collins? I need to bring her a well-thought out plan, not simply bumble out whatever comes to mind. The doctor said you should rest tomorrow, so this will give us something to do."

"Rest isn't an option. Not with everything going on. We need to get to the bottom of things, and the first place we need to go is the bank to get answers about the construction company's account. There has to be something I'm not seeing, and odds are not all the information is filed away in the office. The bank will have everything I need."

Her wide grin quickly melted into a frown. "Are you sure that's a good idea?"

"Positive. I need something concrete to explain this shit so I can pass it along to Deputy Wells. Until then, all we have is speculation of wrongdoing and suspicions. Two things that won't do a damn thing."

"And what about Matthew?"

He sighed and rubbed the back of his neck. "If we don't have more answers by this time tomorrow, we'll fill him in on everything we've found."

"Okay," she said, not sounding sure of his plan. A beat of silence passed before she continued. "You should probably get some sleep. It's late."

His body nearly leapt from the couch at the suggestion, but he wasn't ready to tell her goodnight. To get up and walk away from her. "Let's stay here a little while longer. I want to hear more about your ideas for a shelter."

She shifted, stretching her legs long until her feet brushed against his thigh.

Unable to resist, he cupped her foot in his hand and waited for her smile of appreciation before gently kneading her soft skin as he listened to her describe every last detail of her new dream.

AWARENESS SLIPPED into Laura's consciousness, trickling into a dream she couldn't quite grasp yet didn't want to leave. Dark edges muted the details, but she didn't want the warm and fuzzy feeling encasing her body to vanish.

She was safe. She was protected. She was happy.

Unable to fight it any longer, she blinked open her eyes and her gaze landed on Cade's sleeping face at the other end of sofa. The contentment buzzing through her intensified into some-thing more.

She studied him as moments from the night before came back to her. He'd rubbed her feet and never took his focus from her as she laid out her vision for a women's shelter in Pine Valley.

He'd listened. He'd been engaged. He made her feel valued in a way no one ever had before.

They must have drifted off somewhere between talks of the future and questions about the present. The past had stayed off limit. She was tired of talking about Isaac and terrified of the damage her ex would try to cause when seeking his parental rights. Too nervous to discuss it, she hadn't asked about his past. Even though a hundred questions about the life he'd led outside of Pine Valley, and the ribbon she'd found in the office, sat on the tip of her tongue.

Maybe they didn't need to hash out every detail of the lives they'd lived before now. But she wanted to find a way to show him she understood he'd walked away from something traumatic and dangerous and came out a better person. A person who saw her for who she was and made her want to be better. Not only for her baby, but for herself as well.

An idea formed in her mind, and she snuck off the couch and tiptoed down the hall to the office. The award she'd found was on the desk where she'd left it. This was something special. Something that should be displayed with pride, not thrown back in a drawer for no one to see.

Sending out a quick prayer that Cade wouldn't notice it was gone, she slipped it off the desk and crept into the guest room across the hall where she'd put her bag. She tucked away the medal then made quick work of dressing in fresh clothes and running a brush through her hair before washing away her morning breath in the bathroom.

Satisfied with her appearance—makeup free and with no fear of Cade's response—she went into the kitchen to throw together breakfast. As she pulled eggs and shredded cheese from the stainless-steel fridge and found the right pan and bowls, she couldn't help but think back on other early mornings preparing a meal for a man who slept.

With Isaac, she'd made as little noise as possible, making sure to cook things exactly the way he liked them. It didn't matter that she preferred bacon to sausage links or omelets to scrambled eggs, she created a meal to someone else's preference.

Someone who never once showed appreciation or even kindness at her thoughtfulness.

Cracking the eggs into a bowl, she rolled her eyes. Not thoughtfulness. Fear.

But now, she'd found the ingredients for a simple breakfast she wanted, knowing Cade would be happy with anything she did.

A lightness lifted her spirits. She whirled around to the stove, turning on the burner and heating her pan before pouring the eggs inside.

"Something smells amazing."

She smiled at the sound of Cade's voice then turned around and stifled a gasp, pretending to cough to cover the strangled noise.

Dark stubble covered his jaw, bordering on a beard. His disheveled hair begged her fingers to run through it. Sleep made his eyes heavy, somehow making him look like a sexy teddy bear who needed a hug and not an overwhelmed basket case like it did her. His white T-shirt was wrinkled, and gym shorts hung low on his hips.

She licked her lips then spun back around to the stove before she did or said something she'd regret. "Thanks. Thought I'd make a simple omelet if that's okay?"

"Better than the cold cereal I usually eat."

His bare feet padded against the wood floor. Every nerve ending in her body sensed him—felt him.

He moved closer. The warmth of his body soothing against

her skin as he reached into the cabinet for a glass. "Sorry. Just gonna reach around you a little."

She cleared her throat, determined not to stop staring at the eggs sizzling in the pan. Because if she moved an inch, if she glanced up with his face so close to hers, she'd do something she shouldn't.

"Do you want coffee? Tea?" he asked, taking a step away and filling his cup with water.

"Water would be great." She peppered the now-cooked egg with cheese then folded it over. "How are you feeling?"

"My head hurts but not too bad."

She reached up to grab her own glass from the nearby cabinet just as he stepped into her personal space with the same objective. His hand brushed against hers, causing a rush of heat to trickle from her head to her toes.

"Oh, sorry," she said, turning to give him room.

He pivoted, bringing his chest to press against her.

The world stopped. Her throat went dry. She stared at his chest, watching the place where his heart beat and swore she could see it thudding—beating as rapidly as her own.

"Laura?"

He said her name like a question, pulling her gaze up to his. Their eyes met, and the intensity in his stare threatened to drop her to her knees. She braced a hand against him to steady herself and the heat from before morphed into an inferno.

He wet his lips as he watched her.

Dear God almighty. I'm in trouble.

Without a word, he hooked an arm around her waist and erased any distance between them. He dipped his chin as if asking another question.

A question she understood deep in her soul. A question she only had one answer for.

She lifted herself onto her toes and pressed her lips to his.

Stars exploded behind her closed eyelids. Her core tingled with excitement.

His other arm wrapped around her, and he deepened the kiss. His tongue flicked into her mouth, and she moaned, accepting whatever he could give her.

This was what she'd been missing. Her whole life she'd searched for someone to make her feel loved and cherished and desired. With one simple kiss, Cade had all those feelings whirling inside her, leaving her begging for more.

Pulling away, Cade gripped her hips in his large hands and smiled at her.

Oh no. Had she done something wrong? Had he not wanted to kiss her?

He leaned down and pressed his lips to the center of her forehead before he whispered in her ear, "The eggs are burning."

12

S tanding in the line at the bank an hour later, the taste of her lips still lingered on Cade's tongue. If the assaulting smell of burning eggs hadn't interrupted Cade's kiss with Laura, it would have been impossible to put any distance between them.

Damn eggs.

Only the night before he'd warned himself to take things slow—to not scare her away with the intensity of his feelings. Then she'd shocked the hell out of him by making the first move.

Now, excited energy swirled through his body at high speed. He wanted nothing more than to grab Laura by the hand and haul her back to his house to see all the wonderful places another kiss could lead.

But there were other things he needed to focus on, no matter how difficult.

"Good morning, Cade." The pretty brunette teller flashed him a wide smile and gave a little wave. "What can I do for y'all this morning?"

With Laura by his side, he walked to the open window. He

dipped his chin in greeting. "How ya doing, Brenda? I need to have some statements printed."

Brenda kept her smile, but questions shined behind her thick, black glasses. "You know you can print those out from your online banking, right?"

Cringing, he scratched the back of his neck. "I'm horrible with that stuff." He didn't want to admit he didn't have the information he needed to even log in to the online accounts. Matthew handled all of that.

"Not a problem. Do you just need last month's statement?"

He glanced at Laura with raised brows. "How far back should we look?'

"Look?" Brenda asked. "Is there a problem?"

Laura set a palm on his arm as if sensing his increasing panic at the simple questions being lobbed his way. "Can we get statements going back the last two years?"

Another hooked-brow glance at Cade. "For the company or personal account?"

"Business," he said, clearing the discomfort from his throat.

"That will take a minute or two." Brenda typed on her computer then spared Laura a quick glance before returning her focus on him. "I have to step away to grab the copies. I'll be right back."

The vise in his chest tightened as she walked away. Once he understood what was going on with the botched numbers and mysterious flash drive, he needed to keep better tabs on what was going on at the office. Just because numbers generally pissed him off and he was better with his hands, didn't mean he should be so far removed from the finances.

"Once we get the statements, we can take them back to the office and compare what we see on the flash drive," Laura said. "Maybe we can find more details on the actual billing of clients. Then we can see if the amount billed matches the amount deposited."

"Sounds like you're suggesting embezzlement." He hadn't put the word to the action yet, but the thought of Matthew taking money from their business sat like a boulder in his gut.

They were best friends. If Matthew needed money, he would have done everything he could to help. There was no reason for him to steal, sneak, or lie to get his way.

Unless there were more secrets tangling up this web they'd discovered.

She took his hand and squeezed. "I'm sure there's a reasonable explanation for everything. We need to find it."

Her presence calmed his nerves, and he clung onto her encouragement. No matter the reason, she was right. There was an explanation. He was just afraid of what it was.

Brenda's dangly bracelets announced her return and she handed over the thick envelope. "If you need anything else, I'm always happy to help."

"Thanks." He took the offered envelope then pressed a hand on the small of Laura's back to steer her past the seating area with two black chairs and a tiny loveseat. He always wondered who the furniture was set up for as he'd never actually seen anyone sit on it.

The glass door nestled between two offices opened before he reached it. Her father, Mayor Jenson Metcalf, and his wife, Nicole, stepped inside.

Laura stiffened and froze beside him.

"Well look who it is," Jenson said, his mouth in a tight line, slightly curved on one side.

Nicole extended her arms and engulfed Laura in a hug. "Oh, darling. I'm so happy to see you. It's been too long. And look at you."

Jenson rested a hand on his wife's shoulder and tugged her back to his side. "That's enough, Nicole. No need to cause a scene."

Laura scowled. "She's just hugging her daughter, Dad."

The curve left Jenson's lips, and something darkened in his light blue eyes. "Well, that daughter is already the talk of the town. No need to get more tongues wagging."

Cade's hackles rose. He'd formed his own opinion of Jenson Metcalf at an early age. Coming from a happy home filled with love and respect, it was easy to spot a bully. To feel the oppressive tension smothering the Metcalf house the moment he stepped inside.

His protective instincts kicked in. He took a closer step to Laura and kept his palm flattened against her spine. Jenson might have overlooked him as a kid, not noticed him hiding in the shadows as he berated and emotionally tortured his kids, but Cade always saw him.

Always heard him.

Always knew the monster behind the well-placed mask.

That monster was slipping through the veneer, his sights set on Laura. He didn't care who Jenson Metcalf was, no way he'd allow the man to harm Laura. Wouldn't let him send her into an emotional tailspin with the manipulation and snide comments he aimed like missiles.

He leaned close to Laura's ear, gaze locked on her father. "You okay?"

She nodded.

Jenson snorted. "You think you need to protect her from her own father? It appears she's gotten into more than enough trouble since spending time with you." He kept his voice low, mindful not to let anyone walking by hear the harsh words he spoke with his jovial expression still in place.

"Dad, stop."

Finally, Jenson schooled his features into a sympathetic smile. "I'm just worried about you. You're pregnant and alone and not talking to Isaac. Honey, he's the father of your child and you're spreading rumors that he came after you. You two really need to work this out. You can't do this alone."

Cade waited a couple seconds to give Laura the space and time she needed to answer her father, but when she didn't, he slid his hand from her back to wrap around her waist, hopefully giving her support.

"She's not alone," he said, voice firm and strong. "She has a village around her."

Jenson glared at Cade. "She needs her family. She needs Isaac."

Laura lifted her chin. "I have everything I need. No thanks to you. Come on, Cade."

She grabbed his hand and marched outside.

Pride swelled inside him. He focused on that instead of the soft sniffles of Nicole and his swift desire to put his fist in Jenson's face.

THE SUN BEAT DOWN, intensifying the heat building inside Laura. Tears burned the backs of her eyes. The pressure in her chest hurt almost as much as the ache threatening to split her heart in two. The only thing keeping her from completely crumbling was the feel of Cade's strong hand in hers.

Cade walked past his truck parked outside the bank.

"Where are we going?" she asked, glancing behind her to make sure her parents hadn't followed them outside.

"Let's go for a little walk."

She stopped in the middle of the sidewalk. "What about the statements? And your head? It has to be hurting. I agreed to visit the bank because it wouldn't be too strenuous. The plan was to return to the office—where I'd make you sit and relax as much as possible—then talk you into going back home."

He shrugged. "My head's fine, and the statements can wait. A little fresh air sounds nice."

She studied his face. If he was in any pain, he hid it well.

She wanted to argue and insist they go to the office right away, but he was right. Fresh air did sound nice. A good way to clear her mind from all the crap her dad always managed to jam in there. "Will you tell me if you're hurting at all?"

He grinned. "You bet."

They walked hand in hand through town. She felt the gaze of everyone they passed land on them, but she kept her head high and pretended it didn't matter. Let them look. Let them be jealous of the man who stood beside her and oozed protection and kindness.

A subtle breeze floated down the street, cooling the warm rays of sun and blowing the bottom of her skirt as she walked. She'd rolled her eyes when she'd unpacked her bag and found the red and white summer dress Jude had packed. Thank God it still fit, flowing gently over her growing bump. She'd swept up half her hair and secured it with a clip. The strands left long down her back tickled her neck. Birds flew overhead and talked to each other in joyful chirps and caws.

She sighed.

"What's wrong?" Cade asked, darting his gaze around the town square as if afraid she'd spotted danger.

She flicked her wrist toward the blue sky. "The birds."

"You don't like them?"

His teasing tone made her smile.

"I've always felt like a bird trapped in a cage. Struggling to break free and fly away. First at home with my dad, then with Isaac. I finally walked away from both of them, and I still feel trapped. Still feel like I can't quite fly away from the men holding me hostage."

Cade tugged on her hand and led her to a bench situated on the grassy square. A gazebo sat in the middle of the recently mowed space. He waited for her to sit before settling beside her. He hooked an arm along the back of the bench, shifting to face her. "Is that what you want? To fly away from here?"

She smiled at the worry in his green eyes and rested a palm on his cheek. He still hadn't shaved, and the whiskers scratched her skin.

Much like they had when she'd kissed him. When his stubble had rubbed against her jaw. Confusion stole her words. She'd flown from her father's cage right into Isaac's. Was she merely hopping into Cade's world because she was afraid to be alone? Was her father right, and she couldn't do this by herself, so she'd latched onto the one man who'd shown her thoughtfulness? Had she sought the comfort of yet another man who'd lock her in a cage?

No, Cade would never lock her away and stifle her. Never demand her obedience or try to control her.

Cade would never, ever hurt her.

"I want to be free of the men always trying to hold me back. I don't know if that's ever going to happen. Not with the baby coming. Isaac won't back down, and it looks like my father chose a side." A humorless laugh shot from her mouth. "I'm not surprised he didn't choose my side, and I hate to admit this, but it hurts. Hurts to know that after everything Isaac did to me, my father would still support him. That he'd still champion him. It doesn't make sense."

The tears she'd held back in the bank finally flowed down her cheeks.

Cade brushed them away. "Crazy doesn't often make sense."

She laughed. "You're saying my father's crazy?"

"I'm saying your father's an asshole. I saw how he treated you guys. All of you. Matthew doesn't talk about it much, but I was around. I noticed the thinly veiled threats and the punishments that never fit the crime. Hell, the punishments he doled out for no better reason than to keep you all in line. He's not right, and any father who'd choose a man like Isaac over his daughter is a father who deserves a swift kick in the balls."

"What about this little one's father?" She lifted her hand

from his face and placed it on her abdomen. "If my dad was bad, Isaac will be ten times worse. How do I protect him or her?"

"I meant what I said before. You won't be doing any of this alone." He rested his hand on top of hers and stared at her stomach with such tenderness—such love—she almost melted on the spot. "I'm here for both of you. Whatever you need."

She swallowed hard, wanting so bad to believe him.

Memories of their kiss assaulted her as she savored the feeling of his simple touch. She wanted nothing more than to lean forward and do it again. But not here in the middle of town with every eye that passed aimed their way. "Thank you," was all she could manage to say, emotions getting the best of her.

"Anytime. You ready to head back to the office? The sooner we get through these, the sooner we can find what we're looking for." He waved the envelopes as if she'd forgotten the reason they'd stopped in town to begin with.

And to be honest, for a few moments, she had.

Raising to her feet she nodded, took his extended hand, and walked beside him.

13

C ade sat in the middle of the room, papers scattered around him. The tension at the back of his head increased. He rubbed small circles against his temples and willed the pain to go away.

Not like it helped.

Laura sat at his desk. She clicked through spreadsheets and statements on the computer. "We've been looking at this for hours. Pouring over numbers and data. I can't find any discrepancies in the bookkeeping. It might be time to call Matthew."

He winced, hating what he was about to suggest. "I haven't looked in his office."

She frowned. "Why not?"

"It just seems wrong. That's his personal space, and I guess I was hoping I'd figure out what the hell was on that flash drive and put all the pieces together without having to invade his privacy."

"That makes sense, but I think the time has come to take that step. We have statements and payment information, which is great. The thing I'm missing is billing. I need to see the actual estimates and amount billed for each project. If there's a disconnect, that's where it will be."

Sighing, he stood then squeezed his eyes closed as a wave of dizziness slammed against him.

"Are you okay?" Laura asked, her voice suddenly so close, her steady hand on his back.

He opened his eyes and smiled down at her. "I am now."

She grinned.

Resisting the urge to kiss her again, he tucked a strand of hair behind her ear. Now that she'd opened Pandora's box, he'd have a hard time keeping his hands off her. But he didn't want to move too fast.

"Are you sure you don't want to call Matthew and ask him about everything? He might have a simple answer." Hope shined from her eyes. She nibbled her bottom lip in the way she did when unsure of herself or what she had to say.

Dammit, he wanted to capture that lip in his mouth.

He needed some space before things took a turn that kept them in his office for the rest of the day. He took a step back and raked his hand through his hair. "Not quite yet. Let's head into his office and search for the billing statements. If we can't find what we need, I'll make the call."

Laura offered him a wide smile that didn't quite reach her eyes. "Let's go. I have plenty of experience digging around in Matthew's space. I used to do it all the time as a kid." She winked and led the way out of the room.

Chuckling, he thought back to any incriminating evidence he may have left at Matthew's when he was younger.

Laura flipped on the light in Matthew's office. The dark blue walls matched his own, but Matthew's desk was a light cherry wood with a matching filing cabinet in the corner. Two leather bucket seats sat in front of the desk, a circular table between them with a potted orchid in the middle. Framed photos of past projects hung on the walls, while one from his wedding day sat proudly on the desk.

"Any chance you know where the billing statements are?" Laura asked and settled into the rolling chair in front of the computer. She switched on the laptop then cringed. "Hopefully not on here since we need a password."

He strode across the room to the filing cabinet and opened the top drawer. "We make out the estimates in triplicate. That way we can give the client the exact same paperwork we keep for ourselves. Might be the only actual paper we use in the billing. Everything else is paid and stored electronically."

"Are the estimates given during the bidding process usually pretty close to what's due at the end of the project?" Laura spun the chair to face him.

He tipped his head from side to side. "Pretty close. We've gotten better over the years at giving a more accurate bid. We learned quickly that people get pretty pissed if we charge much more than what we quote for our services."

"And you always keep a copy?"

Nodding, he flipped through the labeled files until he found the one he wanted. He unearthed a jam-packed folder with papers spilling out and laid it on the desk before retrieving another one.

"The more recent quotes will be in this one," he said, dipping his chin toward the one he'd placed right in front of Laura.

She flipped it open then shuffled through the top few pages. "The pantry isn't in here."

He wanted to scream his frustration, but he stuffed it down. "Great. Now we get to sift through all this and see what's missing."

"There's a record of all the company's projects on the computer I've been using. I even set it up in a spreadsheet to make things easier to navigate. I think I sent you the file."

"Let me grab my computer so we can compare everything."

He returned to his office and found what he needed then dragged one of the chairs from in front of the desk to Laura's side. His heart beat at an unsteady pace, but he couldn't be sure if it was because Laura was so close or they were on the right track to finding answers.

The clock on the wall ticked away the seconds. One by one, missing estimates were discovered then noted on a separate spreadsheet. After pouring through the first manilla folder, Cade leaned back in his chair and rubbed his eyes. "I need a break."

Laura straightened the paperwork and placed the file on the edge of Matthew's neat desk. "That's a good idea. We made some progress, and I'm sure there will be a couple more estimates that are unaccounted for. Once we have them all listed, we can see if there are any similarities between the projects."

"Such as?" In his mind, they were standing at the foot of a mountain, staring up at the impossible climb of discovery.

Shrugging, she turned his laptop toward her. "For starters, most of these projects are focused on community builds or expansions. The food pantry, a local park, the police station. I don't see any personal properties on the list. Nothing that's a new build or even one of your larger money-makers."

He rolled the new information around in his head. "That has to mean something. I'm just not sure what."

She ran a finger along the computer screen, eyes narrowed. "I don't see Crossroads Mountain Retreat on here. The estimates we've waded through were from the same time frame when you guys did all that work on the lodge. That's a part of the community, but I'm sure that cost a ton to build."

He nodded, remembering the satisfaction of playing a part in such an important place. A place that would help people like him who'd sworn to serve and protect then needed a place to land for a while. A place to heal. The project had been hard and satisfying as hell—not to mention a good payday.

Laura shifted in her chair, unease showing on her scrunched-up face. "Did my dad help you get that job?"

"I'm not sure. Matthew's the one who took point on that. He never mentioned how he'd met Brooke. Why?"

"Brooke told me she'd spoken to my dad about the pantry. About the fundraising for the remodel. I didn't give it much though until now. Could he be helping Matthew get certain bids around town?"

The information sat like a boulder in his gut. He didn't want Jenson's help with anything, especially getting jobs. Mountaintop Construction had a good enough reputation to get work based on merit.

But that hadn't always been the case. They'd been a new business once, struggling to prove themselves. If Matthew spoke with Jenson about finding projects around the community, what else were the two discussing behind closed doors?

STUNNING VIEWS of the Smoky Mountains welcomed Laura inside the lodge of Crossroads Mountain Retreat. Light spilled through the floor-to-ceiling windows, highlighting the three-story stone hearth in the center of the room. It was too hot for a fire today, but the space was just as cozy with the pockets of deep brown furniture scattered over burgundy rugs.

A tan dog with a smiling face and wagging tail trotted over to greet her and Cade at the giant double doors as they stepped through.

She crouched and scratched the pup under his jaw. "Hey there, Wyatt. How are ya, boy?"

Wyatt's tail wagged even faster.

She stood and waved at Izzy Sterling, the young receptionist who held down the job part-time while also attending school. Laura admired Izzy's resilience and had enjoyed getting to know her during the time she spent here doing odds and ends for Brooke.

"Hey, Laura. What are y'all doing today? Can I help you with anything?"

"We're here to speak with Brooke. She's expecting us."

Wyatt trotted to Cade's side and sniffed his shoes.

Cade chuckled. "Not sure what you're smelling, but good to see you, too." He ran his large hand over Wyatt's back, making Laura more jealous than it should.

As if hearing her name, Brooke emerged from down the hall. "Hi, you two. I found the paperwork you'd asked about. Do you want to step into my office?"

Laura glanced back at Cade, who nodded his agreement. "Lead the way."

Wyatt took her words as an invitation to join them and jogged beside her, nails clacking along the mahogany floors.

Brooke's office was one of the few rooms in the lodge Laura had never visited. Like the lobby, the room showcased the green peaks of the mountains through large windows and a smaller version of the fireplace took up one wall. Black and white photos of different locations at the retreat were placed around the room—the lake that lay beyond the lobby, one of the guests' cabins in the woods, the land cleared for archery and hatchet throwing.

Over the last few months, Laura had visited most of those places. Working for Brooke hadn't simply given her extra cash but given her a sense of purpose and helped her heal. She'd been encouraged to use all the facilities. She'd taken yoga outside to learn how to channel her stress and take care of her body, helped take care of the therapy dogs, and spent countless hours walking trails alone. For once, taking time to focus on herself and what she wanted. What she needed.

Cade's hand on her back as he helped her into a cushiony chair was a sharp reminder of exactly what she wanted.

"Thanks so much for seeing us on such short notice," Cade said, sitting in the chair beside her.

"Of course." Brooke rounded the corner of her desk and pulled a piece of paper from the top drawer. "I found the estimates you asked about. I'm curious about your reasons for wanting to see it."

Laura frowned. "Estimates? Plural?"

Cade leaned forward and grabbed the paperwork. He flipped through the pages. A scowl deepened the V between his eyebrows. "Why do you have more than one?"

Brooke shrugged. "That's what I was given."

Laura glanced over Cade's shoulder and studied the pages. Two separate estimates. All from the same paperwork with the Mountaintop Construction logo. All with Matthew's signature on the bottom.

"This doesn't make sense," Cade muttered. "There's no reason for multiple estimates unless you hired us for a separate project. One not quoted in the first estimate."

As if sensing his anxiety, Wyatt placed his head in Cade's lap and let out a little whine.

Cade continued to mutter but rested a hand on the dog's head and scratched behind his floppy ears.

Brooke shook her head. "No added on or new projects. The lodge was a big build, but the only thing on the property I needed a construction crew to handle."

"Do you remember the time span between being given the two separate estimates?" Laura asked.

"I'm sorry. No." Brooke lifted her hands as if wishing she could offer something more then dropped them to her lap. "That was a few years ago, and that time was so hectic. Between the new build, me working nonstop on the rest of the property, and the craziness that happened with the sex trafficking ring that was uncovered after Izzy's abduction—I'm afraid I can't recall the exact timeline of when I was given paperwork from your company."

"Where do we go from here?" Cade gave the papers a frustrated shake.

Laura rested a hand on his knee, earning a wide-eyed stare from Brooke which she ignored. "You were new to town when you hired Cade and Matthew. How did you hear about their company?"

Brooke swished her lips to the side as if trying to recall specific details. "A lot of people in the community were interested in what I was doing here. Most people knew my grandpa and loved this place when it'd been a children's camp. After I inherited the land and made plans to turn it into a retreat for injured law enforcement and veterans, word spread quick. A lot of folks stopped by to introduce themselves and get as many details from me as they could. Or offer tons of advice I didn't really need." She snorted out a small laugh. "Gotta love small towns."

"So did Matthew come and introduce himself?" Cade asked. "Sounds like something he'd do. If rumblings reached him about a potential client, he wouldn't hesitate to swing by to say hello. Hell, probably brought you a basket of muffins."

Laura smiled. He was right. Matthew was kindhearted and always wanting to make people feel welcome, whether that benefited him or not was beside the point.

Which made his squirrelly behavior the past few days even more puzzling.

"Umm, no, actually. I met the mayor before I met Matthew. He introduced himself while I was in town one day. He gave me Mountaintop Construction's business card and mentioned you were local and did great work."

Laura's stomach dropped. "You also mentioned my dad talked to you about the pantry. About the fundraising."

"That's right. He took a big interest in rallying business owners around town to contribute funds for the renovation. I was more than happy to help in any way I could. Still am."

Cade lifted his hand from Wyatt's head and rubbed the back of his neck. "I had no idea Jenson was so invested in the company. I don't like it."

Neither did Laura. "The real question is what is my dad getting out of this?"

Brooke ping-ponged her gaze between the two of them. "You mean besides promoting his son's work and helping to get community projects funded?"

Laura swallowed her response. There was so much the people of Pine Valley didn't understand about Jenson Metcalf. If there was one thing she knew about her father, he never did anything out of the goodness of his heart. He always had an ulterior motive.

So the big question remained—what was that motive?

14

A call from one of Cade's suppliers added to the increasing tension consuming his entire body and sent him and Laura back into town. The last thing he wanted to do was deal with backordered supplies, but he still had a job to do.

Laura sat beside him on the bench seat of his truck. Tight lines on her pretty face showcased her confusion and worry. She studied the paperwork Brooke had let them take. "If I remember correctly, you received three payments from Brooke during the construction of the lodge. One when she hired you, one halfway through the build, the rest at completion of the project."

He sighed, thinking back on what he remembered on the sea of numbers that had swum through his brain over the last couple days. "Sounds right."

"Those payments add up to the first estimate given, which means we found no records of the second amount from the second statement. We need to figure out where that money is. Maybe another bank account you weren't aware of?"

He lifted one shoulder. "Nothing that'd have my name on it,

which means if there is another account, it's one I don't know about. And more importantly, one I'm not *supposed* to know about."

"The food pantry was also on the list of projects we didn't have estimates for. Mrs. Collins has only made the one payment so far, but she might have some information. Possibly even copies of those estimates we can look at. If nothing else, she can clue us in on any conversations she may have had with my dad or Matthew that don't make sense."

He hated that she'd been dragged into this mess. If she hadn't come in to work for him while Matthew went off to do whatever the hell he did, she'd be out of harm's way. Oblivious to the questions and suspicions brewing in his gut. She had enough on her plate without adding to it from his.

Towering evergreens and patches of maple trees whirled by as he continued down the mountain. He wanted nothing more than to get out of his truck and get lost in nature for the rest of the day. To breathe in the fresh air and wander along trails to gurgling creeks. Maybe discover a waterfall or new vista. Anything but drive into town and deal with the headache of backorders.

Especially when his mind was consumed with so much other shit.

Shit that he couldn't even begin to wade through because he didn't understand it. Or didn't want to understand it because if his instincts were to be trusted, things would be going south very soon with his best friend.

He made the turn that led to the food pantry. He needed to discuss Mrs. Collins' options with her now that the tile she'd ordered wouldn't be available for six weeks. A detail that seemed so trivial at the moment but still needed to be addressed. Then he could talk to her about the missing estimates.

"We'll ask her about it," he said. "Brooke said she'd check

her records to see where the extra payments she made were sent, but Mrs. Collins might have more information at the forefront of her mind. Maybe we'll get lucky." He slid into a parking spot on the side of the road and shut off his engine. It didn't take long for the heat from outside to take over the vehicle once the air conditioning stopped pumping out cold air.

"Fingers crossed," Laura said and slid down from the truck.

He sat for a moment, impressed with her positivity. The world made it so easy to get sucked up in the negative—get weighed down by the darkness.

But not Laura. She was a shining light. A beacon of hope urging him forward and promising something better. Something more.

Something he wanted to keep in his life for good.

A slamming car door stole his attention and snapped him back to the moment. He searched through the windshield for the source of noise and his blood began to boil.

Isaac stalked toward Laura, murder in his narrowed gaze and determined motions.

Shit. Cade jumped out of the truck just as Isaac got to Laura and grabbed her wrist, yanking her to him on the sidewalk.

Laura's eyes were wide. Her mouth slightly parted. She swiveled around until she found Cade. She tried to yank her arm away from Isaac, but he kept her rooted to spot.

Cade stormed forward. "Let her go."

"Stay out of this," Isaac hissed out then pivoted to block him from Laura. "Come on, Baby. Just talk to me. You know I love you. I want us to work this out. We need to be there for the baby."

"Stop. Leave me alone. You and I will never be together again." She pulled back, but Isaac refused to release her.

The sun glinted off something metallic in Isaac's free hand. He maneuvered Laura so her back was pressed against his chest. His hand came up to Laura's side. The blade of a small knife pointed to her ribcage.

Red outlined Cade's vision and the need to get her away from Isaac had him fisting his hands at his sides. She'd already survived so much. This stress and fear weren't good for her or the baby.

Laura let out a long breath and kept her gaze locked on him.

He wanted to reach out, to punch her asshole ex in the face, then figure out a way to keep the sonofabitch away from her forever. But he couldn't move. Couldn't take charge. Couldn't do a damn thing except hope Isaac wouldn't actually hurt the mother of his child—or even the baby inside her.

It took every ounce of effort he had to lift his palms in the air. "Dude, don't do something stupid. Let her go."

Isaac snorted. "You need to leave. I'm here to talk some sense into Laura. Get her to listen to reason and realize she needs to come home. I love her and *our* baby. We're a family, and it's about time she understood that. But she won't stop being stupid and see that with you sniffing around."

"Isaac, please. Don't." Laura's voice trembled. She swallowed hard and cradled her belly with her palm. She inched her hand as close to the knife as she could, as if to create a barrier between the sharp blade and her baby. "You don't want to hurt me or the baby. This won't get you anywhere. Not with me, and not with the law."

He pressed the knife closer to her, burying the tip into the soft cotton of her dress. "Shut. Up. Come with me now, and no one will get hurt."

She winced. "Isaac. Stop."

Cade's phone burned inside his pocket. He needed to get help here before things took a deadly turn. His mind raced as he tried to come up with a plan. He couldn't let Isaac drag

Laura away, but if he made a wrong step, it could lead to disaster.

Like it had before. When his decision had cost the lives of his brothers in arms.

A wave of fear slammed against him, heating him from the inside out.

Isaac put his mouth close to Laura's ear but never took his eyes off Cade. "Say goodbye to your new friend. You won't be seeing him again."

Tears welled in her eyes. Indecision shining brighter than the sun on her face.

A nearby screen door squeaked and slammed against siding. Heavy boots stomped on a worn porch. "I suggest you step away from Laura and put your hands in the air."

Cade turned toward the new voice and relief combined with shock. Mrs. Collins stood on her porch with a shotgun aimed at Isaac.

"Trust me," she yelled. "I have damn good aim. You'll have to let go of her to run to that truck of yours eventually, and when you do, I won't miss. And just in case you don't believe me, you should know police are on the way."

With Isaac's attention fixed on Mrs. Collins, Cade took a small step. Cornered animals made questionable choices, and he didn't want Laura caught in the crosshairs.

"Stupid bitch!" Isaac yelled. "You always get me in trouble. I'm not done with you." He shoved Laura and took off running toward his truck.

Cade shot forward and caught Laura before she hit the cement. He cradled her in his arms as sirens split the air and combined with her soft cries. Whoever was messing with his company might not have targeted Laura the night she'd been attacked, but that didn't mean she was safe.

∾

DESPITE THE HEAT in the old Victorian house, Laura couldn't stop her teeth from chattering. After making sure the knife hadn't even scratched the surface, Mrs. Collins had draped a sage green quilt over her shoulders. Cade sat glued to her side. He ran his palms up and down her arms, but nothing could chase the chill fear had set in her bones.

A soft knock on the doorframe of the sitting room announced a uniformed deputy with a sympathetic smile. "Hi, Ms. Metcalf. I'm here to take your statement."

"Sadie?"

"Deputy Pennel, but you can call me Sadie. I'm sorry this is how we're meeting again."

Laura tried to force a smile for the other woman's benefit but came up empty.

"Please, sit," Cade said, and gestured to the armchair situated beside the loveseat they occupied.

The deputy crossed the room and took a seat before pulling out a small notepad and pen. "We have several deputies, as well as the city police, searching for Mr. Heck. So far, they've come up empty. Is there anywhere you think he might be hiding? Anyone who could be helping him?"

She shrugged. "He only has the one house that's right in town. No other properties. His father died when he was young, and his mother moved away. They're not very close, but he might contact her."

"Do you know her name?"

"Amy Heck. I have her number in my phone if you'd like it."

"That'd be great. What about siblings? Friends? Coworkers?"

Exhaustion made her eyes heavy as adrenaline leaked from her system. She struggled to keep her eyes wide and focused on Sadie. All she wanted was to lean into Cade and close her eyes. Forget for a few minutes that the man she'd once loved had actually threatened her life with a knife.

"He doesn't have any friends and no siblings."

"Coworkers?"

"None he was close with."

Cade cleared his throat and shifted on the cushion, resting a palm on her thigh. "What about your dad?"

She squeezed her eyes closed for a beat against the question. Not because it angered her, but because he'd made a valid suggestion. "Isaac and my father are very close. He works with my dad, and my dad's always championed him. Even pressured me to get back together with him knowing about the abuse I suffered."

Sadie stopped scribbling and raised a well-shaped brow. "There's a history of abuse with Mr. Heck? Have you ever pressed charges before?"

Shame heated Laura's cheeks. She wrung her hands on her lap, avoiding eye contact with everyone in the room. "No."

Cade cupped his hand over hers, stopping the motion of her circling palms.

Calmed by his touch, she blew out a long, shaky breath. "I endured Isaac's abuse for many years. I thought I was hiding it. Thought nobody knew." She let out a humorless laugh. "There wasn't enough makeup in the world to cover all the bruises. To hide the marks and scars. I thought I could change him. Thought he loved me. Isaac doesn't know how to love, and it wasn't until I found out I was pregnant that I knew I had to leave. I have someone else to protect now."

"Making a statement today, you're taking a huge step in protecting both you and your baby," Sadie said. "I've seen this more times than I care to admit. Men like him who've lost control of the women they claim to love. They can't handle it. They make dangerous decisions they can't come back from. Threatening you with a knife is one of those choices. The law will step in and do whatever we can to help you. I promise."

Mrs. Collins stepped into the room carrying a tray filled

with a steaming white teapot and matching teacups. Her red handkerchief tied around her head and well-worn overalls made her look even more petite somehow. "Amen. That boy better not show his face around here again."

That sentiment coaxed the first real smile from Laura. "Thank you again for what you did."

Mrs. Collins set down the tray on the oversized trunk turned coffee table and waved a hand in the air. "I wish I could have done more. And will if he comes back to my house."

Sadie clucked her tongue. "I'll pretend I didn't hear that. But back to what was mentioned about your father. Do you believe he'd help Isaac evade the law?"

Cringing, she nodded. "I wouldn't put it past him."

"And what's your father's name?"

"Jenson Metcalf."

Sadie's brow shot up again. "The mayor?"

"One and the same," Cade said. "Which makes his possible involvement trickier. I don't doubt he'd assist Isaac—the way he defends the guy is nauseating—but his biggest concern has always been his position in the town."

A tiny bit of relief slipped into Laura's limbs. She'd spent so many years thinking nobody outside their home saw who her father really was. That obviously wasn't true, and Cade wasn't afraid to expose Jenson and the monster inside him.

Mrs. Collins made a tsking sound and took the spot on the other side of Laura, sandwiching her closer with Cade.

A spot that made her feel safe and protected.

"A father should always protect his child. Not feed her to the wolves. It's a shame to think there are men out there who care more about perception and status than making sure their daughter's safe. Everybody should have a secure place to land —and not having that from parents is a shame."

Cade bumped his thigh against Laura's, turning her attention his way. "This might be the perfect time to bring up the shelter."

Her stomach churned. He was right, but she wasn't prepared. Hadn't nailed down a precise plan to lay out for Mrs. Collins.

"Shelter?" Sadie asked, perching on the edge of her chair. "Am I missing something?"

Laura shifted to face Mrs. Collins. "I agree with everything you said. I grew up without that safe place, and that's part of what kept me under Isaac's thumb for so long. When I left, I found support that not everyone has in similar situations. I want to help give that support to other women who find themselves dealing with the same thing."

Interest twinkled behind Mrs. Collins' wire-framed glasses. "That sounds like a wonderful mission that a lot of people need."

"I'd like to tackle that mission with you." She held her breath and watched the myriad of emotions play across Mrs. Collins' face.

"With me? How?"

"We could use this house to create a women's shelter."

Mrs. Collins blinked away tears and pressed a hand to her heart. "Oh my. That's not something I've ever considered, but I love the idea. It's only a matter of if it's possible."

Laura's pulse raced. Excitement pumped through her veins, chasing away the lingering fear and fatigue.

"Well," Sadie said and stood. "I think I have everything I need for the moment, and it looks like you two have a lot to discuss. I'll call if I have more questions or if we find Isaac. And not that you asked my opinion, but I love the idea of a local women's shelter. There's not enough support in this area for women in need. I have some experience helping out in shelters and would lend a hand in any way I can if you two move forward with this idea."

"I'll show you out," Mrs. Collins said, jumping to her feet. "Then you and I have a lot to discuss." She winked at Laura then led Sadie out of the room.

Disbelief stole her ability to move, to think, to speak. Amidst the chaos and terror engulfing her entire life, her biggest dream might be coming true.

15

As happy as he was that Mrs. Collins expressed interest in Laura's vision, Cade couldn't shake the tentacles of fear and guilt dragging him down.

Laura slowly faced him, mouth agape. "Did you hear that? She's interested. She wants to talk to me about using her amazing home for a women's shelter."

He forced a tight smile, not wanting to add any of his weight to her slender shoulders. Shoulders already holding way too much.

She frowned. "What's wrong? Are you okay?"

He struggled against how much to confide. How much to share about the turmoil that hadn't stopped brewing in his gut since seeing a knife pressed against her.

Since not being able to do a damn thing to protect her.

Shaking away the vision, he tried to focus on the positive. "I'm fine."

"Don't give me that," she said with narrowed eyes. "Spill it."

Sighing, he hung his head. "I felt so helpless earlier. I just stood there and watched Isaac threaten you. Watched him hurt you. My mind was racing but I couldn't see a way out that didn't put you in even more harm. I was useless."

A light touch on his forearm lifted his head. He stared into Laura's wide, loving eyes. The blue was so bright, so beautiful.

"You would have found a way to stop him." She spoke with so much conviction, he almost believed her.

"You don't know that."

"Yes, I do. Because you're the best man I know. You've done more for me than anyone else ever has. I trust you with my life."

A familiar punch of guilt jabbed him in the gut. "Maybe you shouldn't."

"Why would you say that? Why can't you see what an amazing person you are? I've known it since I was a little girl, showering you with those silly flowers and weeds I picked in the woods. All I ever wanted was for you to notice me. Even then, I knew being in your life would be the most wonderful thing."

The faces of the men in his unit who'd lost their lives flashed in his mind. Their lives all snuffed out because of him. Emotion clogged his throat. The burden he'd carried around for so many years suddenly was too much—too heavy. "I'm not as good as you think I am. My past is filled with..." he lifted his hands then let them fall as the words failed to come.

"Pain? Trauma? Mistakes?"

He nodded as each suggestion hit him like a missile. "All of that. My choices led to the death of good men. *My actions* led to the deaths of good men. It's my fault. All my fault." Unshed tears burned against the backs of his eyes. He balled his hands into fists and rubbed them up and down his thighs over and over.

She sat still beside him and gave him the space he needed to catch his breath. A few moments of silence passed before she rested a hand over his fist, stopping the frantic motion before he rubbed a hole through the denim. "I understand self-blame. I understand taking on guilt that's not yours to take. I also understand sometimes it's impossible to let go of those things even when logic tells us everything wasn't your fault. I might not know what happened—and you don't need to tell me unless you want to—but I do know you didn't kill those men."

A wall of heat slammed against him, and the smell of the dry desert invaded his senses. The rumbling sound of tanks on gravel roads vibrated his ear drums. A flash of light followed by an explosion...screaming...silence. "I didn't follow my gut. I didn't trust my instincts. I should have turned back. Shouldn't have kept going down that road."

Her palm fought through his clenched fist until she twined her fingers in his. "You couldn't have known what would happen."

"I sensed it. That should have been enough."

Laura wrapped her arms around him and drew him close. She rubbed small circles on his shoulder and pressed her lips to his temple.

No words would ever absolve him of everything he carried, but the comfort and support from Laura melted some of the guilt gnawing at his conscience. Hell, just letting some of his story trickle out loosened the vise that had tightened his chest since the day he'd left the Army.

"Thank you," he whispered into her ear before pulling back enough to see her face. "I didn't want to make this about me because it's not. You're the one who was dealt a horrible blow today."

She flattened a palm to his jawline. "Never apologize for sharing. I want to know you. All of you."

Unable to stop himself, he leaned forward and captured her mouth in his. She tasted like hope—like home. How had she been under his nose all this time? Always a stone's throw away but always too far to touch.

But not anymore.

Now that he'd found her, there was no way he'd ever let her go.

~

LAURA MELTED AGAINST CADE, savoring the feel of his lips on hers. His hands framed her waist, his fingers skimming her sides. Her skin tingled as anticipation zipped through her body. Her core burned, urging her closer. Demanding she erase any space between them.

The first kiss in the kitchen with Cade had been sweet and tentative and filled with nerves. But this...this was so much more. As though all the walls had been destroyed, leaving them both desperate to take things further.

Never had she imagined she'd feel like this. That she could fall so hard and so damn fast. Yes, she might have held a childhood crush, but her wildest dreams couldn't have predicted the depth of her feelings for the man Cade had become.

"Oops, looks like I'm walking in on something." Mrs. Collins' chuckle followed her into the room.

Biting back a groan, Laura broke the kiss but stayed close to Cade.

He hooked an arm over her shoulders, and she snuggled against him.

"There's been all kinds of excitement today." Mrs. Collins grinned and took the chair Sadie had occupied moments earlier. She poured herself a cup of tea then leaned back, eyes alive with interest. "Before we get to any of the good stuff, tell me how you're feeling, Laura. I'm sure what happened earlier with that troubled young man was quite a shock."

Her stomach turned at the mention of Isaac. "I shouldn't be surprised that he'd do something so rash, but I am. Don't get me wrong, I'm used to his violence and anger. But a knife? And where did he plan to take me? Just go back to his house and I'd dutifully stay?"

Cade curled his fingers around her arm, pulling her closer. "You don't have to think about the what ifs. He's not coming anywhere near you again."

She wished she could believe that. But dealing with Isaac had never been simple. Even if there'd been witnesses to his threat and the police were now searching for him. He always found a way to wiggle out of trouble.

"To be honest, I don't want to talk about him right now," she said.

"Then we'll move on." Mrs. Collins took a sip of her tea then set her cup back on the tray. "Maybe we can discuss this idea you have."

Laura wanted to jump in and discuss the possibility of a women's shelter, but that wasn't what had brought them over to visit Mrs. Collins in the first place. "We'll get to that in a second, but first we had some things we needed to talk about regarding the renovation."

She frowned. "But they haven't even started yet."

Cade unhooked his arm from around her and leaned forward, resting his forearms on his knees. "The tile you picked out for the kitchen is on backorder. It will push everything back a few weeks. I need to know if you'd like to choose something in stock or wait."

"I guess that depends on what other decisions I'll be making about the house." The older woman aimed a pointed glance at Laura.

She couldn't help but smile.

Cade gave a long, slow nod. "Fair enough. Which leads me to the next thing."

"There's more?" Mrs. Collins asked, brows raised.

"Unfortunately," Cade said. "Do you happen to have the

estimate you were given from Mountaintop Construction? I don't have one at the office."

"I'm sure I have it around here somewhere." She waved her hand in the air as if the paperwork would manifest in the cozy room.

"Do you remember if you were given more than one estimate?" Laura asked.

Mrs. Collins nodded. "Two, actually. One from Matthew, the other from your father."

Cade went back to balling his hands into fits. "Jenson Metcalf gave you an estimate from our company?"

"Yes. He headed up the community fundraising, which was super helpful in securing the money for the project. The estimate he gave me was the amount left to be paid once the fundraising was done."

Laura tried to wrap her mind around what Mrs. Collins was saying, but it didn't add up. "So you got one estimate from Matthew with the total for the renovations. And then another with the amount still owed after local businesses contributed to fundraising?"

Mrs. Collins nodded. "That's right."

"Weren't you confused as to why you were given two different amounts to pay?" Cade asked.

She shrugged. "Not really. It seemed fair that if the community was contributing, I should make up the difference."

Laura wanted to wrap the woman in a hug. She hadn't realized she'd been duped into spending more money than was owed. "Can we see the paperwork you were given?"

"Sure. Give me a minute to run up to my office and find it."

Once she left the room, Cade sighed. "That doesn't even make sense. She thought Matthew would give her an amount to pay then your father would provide a separate amount because his fundraising efforts didn't cover the extra cost?"

"I've heard stranger schemes." The news was always full of

people who'd fallen for sketchy scams. "Why would she question what the mayor—the father of one of the construction company owners—gave her? Especially when he's spouting nonsense about fundraising and helping her pay for the project."

"Brooke mentioned your father collecting funds for fundraising at the retreat as well. Do you have any knowledge about the nonprofit he represents?"

She shook her head. "Isaac's the one who works for him at the mayor's office, not me. I'd try to step in and do things around town, but Dad only wanted me to look pretty and stand around with my mom at town events. Isaac's the one who's always with Dad. Learning and being groomed by him."

Cade snorted. "It's not exactly like we can ask Isaac about any of this, and I'm not sure about involving your dad. I don't trust him, either. Not when he's been poking around my business, and I wasn't even aware."

"The big question now is if Matthew knows what our dad's been doing. I think it's time we clue him in on what's going on." She bit into her thumbnail as she waited for Cade's response. She'd wanted to bring Matthew in from the beginning but had respected Cade's need for answers.

Cade scrubbed a hand over his face. "Fine. After we talk to Mrs. Collins, we'll stop by Matthew's place. This isn't a conversation I want to have over the phone."

A knot of anxiety tightened her insides. It was past time to discuss everything with Matthew, and she hoped he was as confused about everything as they were. Because if he wasn't, then their problems just got even bigger.

16

Cade sent off a text to Matthew then studied the estimates Mrs. Collins had handed over. His eyes felt like crossing. After their discussion, he wasn't surprised by what he read. But it didn't make it any less troublesome to see in print.

"Are either of you going to tell me what's going on?" Mrs. Collins had sat back in the armchair and tucked her short legs beneath her.

"I wish I knew what the hell was happening. Each second, my head is spinning more and more." Needing to expel some nervous energy, he pushed to his feet and walked around to the back of the couch.

The old floors creaked under his weight. He'd give anything to spend the afternoon combing through the books lining the built-in shelves instead of tackling problems. But he couldn't bury his head in the sand.

"Why don't you start at the beginning?" Mrs. Collins followed him with her gaze. Her pinched expression displayed both her concern and confusion. "Sometimes talking things through from A to Z can help find the missing pieces."

He stopped behind the couch and gripped the edge. "Laura found a flash drive at the office. We think that's why she was attacked."

"So not Isaac?" Mrs. Collins asked.

Laura snorted. "As you've witnessed, he's not exactly one to hide his face when going after me."

Mrs. Collins reached out and squeezed Laura's hand. "He'll get what's coming to him. They always do. I'm so sorry you were there when someone broke in to get this doodad Cade's talking about. But what's on this thing? Why would someone want it?"

He struggled not to laugh at her description of the flash drive. "Spreadsheets filled with numbers I couldn't make heads or tails of, but Laura figured out they were related to past project payments. From there we've discovered missing estimates, as well as involvement from Jenson Metcalf that I never knew about. He shouldn't be talking to our clients at all, and I can't help but feel he's up to something."

He held his tongue about Matthew's possible involvement. He'd talk with his partner soon enough. But one thing was certain, Jenson had overstepped by speaking with his customers.

"Mrs. Collins, you've lived in this town a long time," Laura said, cutting into the mounting tension smothering the room. "Have local businesses always been asked to donate to projects that benefit the town?"

"Honestly, I wouldn't know the answer to that. I've never owned a business, and any place I've worked in the past wouldn't have filled me in on that sort of information. There are plenty of other people who could have answers, though. Mrs. Crawley over at Crawley's Confections has been there for decades, and Bob Truly who owned the hardware store."

"What about payments?" Cade asked. "When Jenson gave you the second estimate, did he mention where to send the check?"

"If I remember correctly, the estimates indicate who to make the check out to." A beat of silence passed as Mrs. Collins wrung her hands in her lap. "Are you saying the community outreach fund is a fraud?"

"Not necessarily," Laura said, drawing out the words. "My dad is too smart to just feed funds from a well-known fundraising effort into his bank account. He'd need a way to get his hands on the money that would fly under the radar. Like using another company to clean the cash."

Cade tightened his grip on the couch. Nothing could ever be simple. "We'll get to the bottom of this. I just hope no one else gets hurt before we do."

Mrs. Collins blew out a long breath. "That's good to hear. Because without seeking more funds from the community outreach program, I'm not sure we could move forward with the shelter. I wouldn't have the resources to do many more changes to this place. Especially with already being financially committed to the updates for the food pantry."

"I don't think there's much that really needs changed," Laura said. "Women who need shelter want a warm, safe place to stay. There's plenty of space here. Rooms to sleep in, space for support group meetings or designated times to get together, and a soon-to-be amazing kitchen to share a meal and heal together."

Mrs. Collins nodded as Laura poured out her vision. Listening to her enthusiasm helped loosen some of the knots in Cade's stomach. He rested his hands on her shoulders, kneading gently while her excitement built with each word— each idea. Timing was everything in life, and this opportunity had swept in right when Laura needed it most.

Gave her something to focus on instead of her fear and uncertainty.

Fear and uncertainty he wanted to protect her from,

allowing her the chance to focus only on the joy and happiness ahead.

As Laura wound down, Mrs. Collins dabbed the corners of her eyes with a tissue. "My dear. What you've just described is beautiful. I would love nothing more than to use my home as safe place for women and children in need. To protect and love and comfort anyone who comes through my door."

He finally rounded the sofa and sat next to Laura, shifting to face Mrs. Collins. "I've already told Laura I'll do anything I can to help, and I know other people in town will, too."

She beamed. "I can't wait to get started. Sounds like we all need to sit down and make some solid plans very soon."

His phone vibrated in his pocket. He pulled it out to find a message from Matthew.

I'm in town. Can meet you at the office in ten minutes?

Ready or not, it was time to confront his business partner. He just hoped when all was said and done, he'd get answers and still have his best friend.

A WHIRLWIND of emotions had Laura's head spinning as she climbed out of Cade's truck. The last couple hours had brought terror, confusion, and excitement. Her mind couldn't comprehend how it was possible to ping pong between so many different feelings.

And now that she was steps away from seeing her brother, she could add anxiety to the mix.

Cade hurried around the front bumper. He fell into step beside her and rested a hand on the small of her back. "You ready?"

"I think so."

He opened the door, waiting for her to step inside before

following. The blast of cool air beat back the heat of the day and sent goosebumps skittering over her bare arms.

"Matthew?" she called out to the empty reception area.

Shattering glass from down the hall was the only response.

Heart racing, she turned wide eyes to Cade. "What was that?"

"Sounds like it came from one of the offices." He maneuvered her to stand behind him and took a few steps down the hall. "Matthew? Is that you?"

"Back here!"

Her pulse slowed and she followed Cade to Matthew's office. The file she'd left on the corner of his desk laid open, papers scattered all over. The framed picture of Matthew and Brandon was across the room. The glass shattered on the ground.

Matthew's sandy blond hair stood out like he'd been running his hands through it all day. His navy-blue t-shirt was wrinkled with stains trickling down the front. The stubble over his normally smooth face made him look disheveled and unkempt.

She let out a small gasp and slipped her hand in Cade's. "What in the world?"

Matthew zeroed in on their joined hands. "What that hell is that?" He spat out the words on a wave of fury and slashed his finger through the air before aiming it in their direction.

Lifting his chin, Cade tightened his grip. "I'll answer whatever questions you have about me and Laura as soon as you explain why you're trashing your office and look like death."

Mathew glared. "So there's a *you and Laura*? What the hell, man. You didn't even want her here and now you're a thing? Are you nuts? That's my baby sister. You've known her since she was a kid."

The well-aimed arrow landed straight in the middle of her

chest. She flinched and swallowed the reaction sitting on the tip of her tongue.

Cade swung their palms up and kissed her knuckles before pressing his lips to her temple. "I'm here for Laura any way she wants me. But that's not the issue right now."

"Oh really? Then what's the issue?"

The anger radiating off her brother stole her senses for a moment. The way he yelled, the tight lines on his face, reminded her so much of her father.

But this wasn't her dad. This was Matthew, and something really major must be happening to turn him into this disaster in front of her.

"Matthew, stop," she said, keeping her voice as calm and steady as she could despite the tremors shaking her insides. "We need to talk about everything that's happened."

Concern wrinkled his brow, transforming him back to the brother she loved. "Shit. Yeah. I'm so sorry about the break-in. I wish to hell you wouldn't have gotten caught up in that."

"That's just the beginning, man." Cade tugged her forward and ushered her into a chair. He stood behind her and crossed his arms over his chest. "I had a break-in at my house last night, too."

"What? Dude, why didn't you tell me?"

"I didn't feel like I could."

Matthew worked his jaw back and forth, as if unwilling to show how much Cade's admission hurt him.

"We think it's connected," she said. "That someone was looking for something in the office then at Cade's house."

Matthew dropped into his desk chair. Sitting across from him, she could see how bloodshot his eyes were. He propped his head up with his fist. "That doesn't make sense. We have nothing to steal here. And it's not like your place is packed with cash. Besides, what does that have to do with someone going through my shit?" Matthew swiped up the papers on his desk then let them fall back down.

The drip of sarcasm took her back, and she swiveled around to gauge Cade's reaction.

Cade rested a reassuring hand on her shoulder and gave a tiny nod, letting her know he'd handle things.

"We couldn't find some paperwork," Cade said, voice hard. "We hoped to find it in here, but only ended up with more questions."

Matthew rolled his eyes. "Would you spit it out already?"

Her jaw dropped. "Matthew. What's wrong with you? We're trying to explain everything."

"Explain what? Your lack of respect of for my privacy? You hooking up with my best friend while carrying another man's baby? I mean, there's a ton that needs explaining so take your pick."

Cade took a step forward. "Enough. You don't talk to her like that. Ever."

Appreciation for Cade mixed with horror at Matthew's words, burning the backs of her eyes. For the first time, she had a man who stood behind her and lifted her up. Demanded others treat her with respect.

But she finally realized she didn't need someone else to speak for her. She was tired of men—even the ones she loved—thinking they could demean her. Thinking they could say whatever came to mind and she was supposed to just sit and take it.

"Cade has been here for me over the last few days while you've been off doing God knows what. I've been helping your business partner—your best friend—figure out what the hell's going on with *your* business while trying to figure out my own life. While struggling not to fall apart after the father of my baby—your niece or nephew—shoved a knife against my side."

Matthew shot to his feet, eyes wide. "Oh my God. Are you

okay? Did he hurt you? I swear I'll find that asshole and finally put my fist in his face."

Although she didn't want her brother upset, relief loosened the tightness in her neck seeing him acting a little more like his protective self and not a jackass. "The police are looking for him now, and if it weren't for Cade and Mrs. Collins, I might be with him. Scared to death. So stop with the attitude."

He sighed and rubbed the back of his neck. "You're right. I'm sorry. I'm not myself. There's no excuse. I should have been around, and I'm glad Cade was there when you needed him. Even if I don't understand what's happening with you two."

Since she wasn't sure what was happening between her and Cade, she decided to dive right into the reason they were here. "Did you know Dad was passing out estimates to your clients?"

Color drained from his face. "You're joking right?"

"Nothing funny about it," Cade said. "We know for a fact he gave estimates to both Brooke Mather and Mrs. Collins. Each with our logo and your signature. Both projects connected to the Community Outreach Fund."

Matthew shook his head over and over as if the constant motion would erase the truth. "No. There has to be a mistake."

"No mistake," Laura said. "Does Dad talk to clients for you?"

Matthew shrugged. "Does he pass out our business card to people he meets who need a contractor? Sure. But that's it."

"What about passing out estimates or discussing payments with the Community Outreach Fund?" Cade asked. "I thought we handled all of that. That the donations came to us, and we figured out additional pricing from there. All of which should be reflected in the one, and only, estimate we give to the clients."

Matthew scrunched his nose. "Yeah. That's how it should be."

"There's a difference between how it should be and how it

is," Laura said, hating the turmoil rolling around in her stomach. Something wasn't right. Mathew was acting cagey, which was so unlike him. She wanted to shake him.

His narrowed eyes were so sad it gutted her like a knife. "Things don't always go the way they should in life." A text message signaled on his phone, and he glanced at the screen. "I gotta go."

She watched in disbelief as Matthew stood and stormed out of the office without uttering another word. She wasn't sure if he was telling the truth about what he knew about their father, but one thing was for certain.

Matthew had a secret.

17

Early evening swept in with the warm breeze. The bright sun moved across the sky, casting long shadows along the land as it hovered above the mountains. Cade carried Laura's duffle bag and waited for her to unlock her front door.

"I want to grab a few more things to take to your place." Laura pushed open the door and flipped on the lights. "As long as you're sure it's okay I stay with you until Isaac is caught."

"Is that even a question?"

Glancing over her shoulder, she shrugged. "I don't want to overstep."

"Never. Where do you want your bag?"

"Down the hall. My room's on the right. I'll gather some of my toiletries from the bathroom really quick."

He padded down the hall behind her. He didn't want to say it, but he couldn't imagine being in his home without Laura—regardless of Isaac's whereabouts. The last couple days had opened his eyes to everything he'd been missing in his life.

Laura had opened his eyes and his heart.

Matthew's reaction to seeing the two of them together

reminded him of why he'd been hesitant to act on the feelings he'd had for her for so damn long. Well, that and the fact she'd still been with Isaac. Even if he hated the choice she'd made to be with such a jackass, he'd never have crossed the line and made a play for someone who wasn't available.

All that was out the window now. Isaac was gone from the picture, and as much as he didn't want to upset his best friend, he wanted Laura more.

Flipping on the bedroom light, his heart sank. A neatly made bed rested against the far wall and a scarred wooden dresser on the other. No frills or decorations. The bare essentials and nothing more.

He wanted to give her more. To fill her room and home with silly pillows he didn't understand, and frames displaying beautiful memories. He wanted her to have a nursery with all the things he never knew kids needed but his sisters always had—like a wipe warmer and the weird shaped pillow they used when feeding their babies.

She shouldn't have to skimp, shouldn't have to worry.

He wanted to give her the world.

"Penny for your thoughts." Her silky voice skimmed the back of his neck.

He set her bag on the ground at his feet and pulled her into his arms. She was a perfect fit. "Just thinking about you and me. About what's started between us the last few days. About how much I've always wanted this, even if I was too scared to admit it to myself."

She pulled away enough to look up and study his face. Her full lips were turned downward, brow furrowed. "Is that so? Then what was all that stuff Matthew said? How you didn't even want me around?"

He cringed as his earlier argument with Matthew came back to slap him in the face. Needing to fully explain himself, he led her to the edge of the bed and sat beside her. "When

Matthew first mentioned wanting you to help out in the office, I was adamant I didn't want you working for us."

She frowned. "I guess that clears up everything. Thanks for your honesty."

"What Matthew didn't know," he pressed on, "was that I'd worked for years to hide my feelings for you. Seeing you every day, being so close to you, would be torture. I'd gotten so damn good at keeping distance between us. Only speaking with you when I couldn't avoid it. No way to do that with you sitting at the reception desk."

The corners of her mouth curled up. "I'm not sure I believe that. I've known you forever. You've always ignored me. Even when I was a kid."

"When you were a kid, you were a little annoying." He grinned.

She rolled her eyes but couldn't hide her amusement. "Maybe a little, but man, I wanted to get your attention so bad. I always picked you flowers. I was such a dork."

He used his index finger and thumb to measure an inch.

She opened her mouth in mock outrage.

He laughed. "You were like a little sister to me."

She wrinkled her nose.

"But," he said, lifting a hand to stop her reaction. "When I came back from the service, I saw you and fell hard. I hated that you were with Isaac and would have given anything to kick his ass. I tried to stay out of your way, but it wasn't easy. Not when all I wanted was to whisk you away and give you a better life. To see the smiling, laughing girl who picked me flowers. Who was carefree and sweet and always thinking of others over herself. You're still that girl. Still putting others above yourself. But you deserve to be put above all else."

"Does that mean you want to stay in my life even after Isaac is caught and everything's back to normal? I mean, once the excitement fades, you might get tired of me. When I don't need someone to protect me or rescue me, the novelty of what we've found might wear off." She issued the words in a light, teasing tone, but uncertainty danced in her eyes.

"You don't need to be rescued. You've already rescued yourself. All I want is to stand beside you, give you someone to lean on when things get tough. If that's what you want, too." He'd been so consumed with what their future looked like, he hadn't considered maybe she had a different plan. He needed to know how she felt as much as he needed his next breath.

"What about the baby?" She rested her hand on her stomach, eyes latched on his. "You might be able to love me someday, but can you love another man's child?"

He swallowed past the lump in his throat. "No matter what the future holds for me and you, I will always love this child."

He was surprised at how true his statement was. He was blessed to have nephews and nieces, but nothing compared to the fierce protectiveness and love that squeezed his chest when he pictured the little bundle that would soon be in this world.

"How can I feel so lucky when so much bad stuff is happening around me?" Laura asked.

"You've been dealt a rough hand for quite a while. It's about time you've gotten some luck."

She smiled up at him before pressing a quick kiss to his lips.
Ding Dong
She froze.

"Expecting company?" he asked.

She shook her head. "You don't think Isaac would be stupid enough to come here and ring my doorbell, do you?"

"He's definitely an idiot," Cade said, standing. "But I'm not sure even he'd do that. Just to be safe, I'll go check it out."

He hurried down the hall, pulse racing. Too much had happened to stay calm until he knew for certain a threat didn't wait on the other side of the door. A quick peek out the front window told him no one waited to ambush him or Laura, but shock still slowed his motion as he opened the door and found himself staring at Nicole Metcalf.

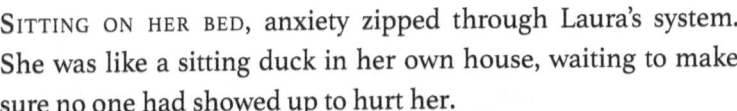

SITTING ON HER BED, anxiety zipped through Laura's system. She was like a sitting duck in her own house, waiting to make sure no one had showed up to hurt her.

Not like that wasn't familiar. She'd spent years not feeling safe in her own home. But she'd made the choice to leave— finally took that first and dangerous step away from her abuser. Her little house might not be flashy, but it had given her shelter and security like she'd never known before.

But now she was back to square one. Waiting. Scared. In danger.

"Laura!" Cade called. "Your mom's here."

She shot to her feet and hurried to the living room. Her mother stood with her hands clasped in front of her, red-rimmed eyes wide and her blond hair pulled in a low ponytail. "Mom? What are you doing?"

Nicole erased the distance between them and wrapped her in a quick hug. "I heard about what happened earlier. I'm just sick. I needed to make sure you were all right."

Laura breathed in the familiar scent of her mom's floral perfume mixed with the lavender lotion she always slathered all over. Her mother had always been warm and caring, a calming force in a house filled with tension.

Until her father came home.

Then she transformed into a meek, trembling woman who'd lost her voice. Lost her sparkle.

As much as she loved her mom and understood she protected her and her siblings the only way she knew how, Laura wanted better for her own child. Wanted a home filled with nothing but love and happiness and laughter.

"I'm fine," she said, taking a step away from her mom.

"You should come home with me until Isaac is found. No need to put yourself in danger."

"I'm with Cade. Isaac won't get his hands on me." Cade might feel guilty that he hadn't been the one to send Isaac running before, but she trusted him with her life. He'd never let anyone hurt her.

"You can't possibly plan to have Cade stay here with you until this is over. Do you know how that looks?" Nicole dropped her voice to a whisper as if even saying the words would invite judgment.

Laura lifted her chin. "It looks like a good man is protecting me. Is wanting me to be safe."

Cade dropped his gaze to the floor, but not before she saw his smile.

"We all want you to be safe, dear. Please. Let your father and me handle this. Your father is beside himself. He only wants to clean up this whole mess."

She snorted. "And how does he want to do that? By glossing over the fact the man he wants me to be with held a knife against my side? Against our baby?"

Nicole cast a nervous glance at Cade before looking back at Laura. "You know your father loves you. He wants what's best for you and the baby."

A dagger through the heart would have hurt less. "What's best for me and my baby is being safe. Is not living with a man who hurts me. Is to raise this child where he or she is always safe. Always loved."

"I've loved you since the first moment I laid eyes on you. I wanted nothing more than to protect you and your siblings. I know..." Another quick look at Cade swallowed the rest of her voice.

A familiar pang of sympathy softened her. She understood how hard it was to leave, and she didn't have three children to support. Her mother never spoke out against Jenson's behavior, but she'd stepped between him and her children countless times. She took his anger to save her kids. Her mom was like a lot of women in abusive relationships. She didn't think she had any other option, so she stayed.

Cade cleared his throat, drawing her attention. "Why don't I grab some water for everyone? Maybe some snacks to pick at? Laura, you haven't eaten in a while."

His consideration warmed her down to her toes. "Thank you."

Once he was in the kitchen, she struggled to line up her thoughts in a way to make her point but not offend her mom. "I know you love me and want what's best for me. I love you, too. But I don't believe that's what Dad wants, or ever has. He wants me to be with Isaac for whatever reason—I don't know, maybe they understand each other in some sick way only two abusers can."

Nicole winced and backed into the edge of the sofa, lowering herself as if her legs couldn't hold her any longer. She shook her head, staring at Laura with her mouth slightly agape.

Laura ignored the tightness in her chest and hurried to sit beside her mom. She took her hands and squeezed them in her lap. "We've never discussed what Dad put us kids through, and Lord knows I don't know everything you've had to endure over the years. I don't need to know."

Tears sprang to the corners of Nicole's eyes. She sniffed, the tip of her nose reddening.

"You need to hear me when I say I know you love me and did your best. But I want better for my baby." She took their joined hands and placed them on her stomach. "This is your grandchild. I want to protect this child from everyone. I won't stay with a man who will hurt me because Dad wants good optics. What he should want is Isaac behind bars and his daughter happy and healthy. Can you understand that?"

Nicole nodded and finally let the tears fall down her face. "I want that to. I'm trying to make everyone happy and it's just not possible. I always let someone down. I always fail somehow."

All Laura wanted to do was shove away her own issues and tackle the insecurities shackling her mother to a man who treated her like dirt.

The same insecurities that had haunted her for as long as she could remember.

But she couldn't save her mother. She could offer her support and love, but she needed to focus on her own journey right now. Because as much as she hated to admit it, she wasn't anywhere near out of the woods.

"You didn't fail, Mom. You've done a damn good job. Maybe it's time for you to start thinking about what's best for you. What you need out of life."

Nicole straightened and yanked her hands away from Laura, as if finally speaking the truth had hit a nerve. "This isn't appropriate," she said, sniffing back all traces of tears. "I came here to see if your father and I could offer you a safe place to stay. Not get into a conversation about me or my marriage."

Laura struggled to keep her face pleasant. "Fine. I appreciate the concern, but I'm good. Cade is more than capable of keeping me safe."

As if on cue, Cade returned carrying a wooden tray filled with three glasses and a plate with cheese and crackers. He set the tray on the coffee table then stood at Laura's side.

A ding sounded from inside Nicole's purse, and she fished out her phone. Standing, she returned the device to the bag. "I'm sorry. I have to go."

It took every ounce of self-control for Laura not to roll her eyes. No doubt her father had told her mother it was time to leave. She rose and gave her mom another hug then walked her to the door.

Nicole hesitated in the doorway and locked her gaze on Cade. "Don't let anyone hurt one hair on her head."

"You have my word."

When Nicole was gone, Laura sighed and sank back down on the couch. She couldn't save her mother, couldn't take on that burden. She'd broken the cycle of abuse and saved herself, and if it came down to it, she'd protect her own child with her dying breath.

18

L aura almost laughed as she pulled items out of the bag she'd hastily thrown together before leaving her house and coming to Cade's. She'd hoped to take her time and bring things that she not only needed but would boost her confidence a bit.

Her mother's unexpected visit had squashed that.

Now she prayed she could squeeze into the t-shirt and leggings she'd stuffed in the bag. At least the shorts and sleep tank fit, even if the silly material clung to her belly. Cade had been nothing but thoughtful and sweet about her pregnancy, but a sliver of insecurity lingered.

She placed the items on the neatly made bed. The guest room in Cade's house was so cozy, it practically wrapped her in a warm hug. A red and black plaid comforter covered the queen-sized bed. Giant pillows begged for her to lay her head on them. A fuzzy, cream-colored rug centered the room and framed mountain landscapes hung on the walls.

All that was missing was a calico cat curled in front of the fireplace.

"Have everything you need?"

She turned at Cade's deep voice. He leaned against the doorframe, arms crossed and the whiskers on his face longer than she'd ever seen. Black joggers hung low on his hips and his gray T-shirt showed off the muscles underneath.

"I think so. Just taking my clothes out so they don't get wrinkled." She wasn't sure how long she'd be at Cade's, so she'd brought enough clothes to get her through a few days. Picking up a shirt, she folded it then placed it on the pile she'd already started.

He moved into the room, the force of his energy enough to suck the air from her lungs. "You can put your things in the dresser."

His suggestion made her giddier than it should.

"You sure?" she asked, taking more from her bag.

"Absolutely. It'd be silly not to."

Grinning like a lunatic, she moved the pile of clothes into the dresser drawers until she'd emptied the bag. She swiped her hand inside to make sure she'd unpacked everything. The medal she'd snuck in there earlier came to the surface and she stiffened.

Cade took a step closer, glancing over her shoulder. "What's that?"

She cringed. She could own up to what she'd planned or feign ignorance and hope he'd laugh about the misunderstanding.

But he wouldn't buy her bullshit, and she didn't want to have any lies between them.

She picked up the gold medal and ran her fingertips along the broad, blue ribbon. "I found this in your office."

He clenched his jaw, questions clear in his green eyes.

Fear threatened to steal the rest of her words. Instinct made her want to recoil—to throw up her arms to protect herself from whatever attack was coming her way.

She sucked in a deep breath. This was Cade. This wasn't

Isaac. He would never, ever hit her. She simply needed to be honest and explain herself.

"I don't know what you did to deserve this, but I know it had to be brave and required courage. You've opened up a little. Told me you made mistakes and people were hurt. But you must have done something much more than that, and I hated to see this medal celebrating you being tossed aside like it didn't matter. Because it does matter. You, and what you did, matter. So I wanted to surprise you by making something special. By turning this into something to celebrate."

He shook his head, gaze cast downward. "I shouldn't have gotten a damn medal. I'm no hero. Never was and never will be."

She rested a hand on his chest, his heart thumping like crazy under her touch. "You're a hero to me. You've shown me kindness and compassion. You've protected me and stood beside me. You're supporting my dream and building me up—showing me that I can do anything I put my mind to. Without you, I don't know where I'd be right now."

He finally looked at her. "You're stronger than you think. You didn't need me to realize that."

"You're right," she said, lifting her chin. "I am stronger than I ever imagined, but you've helped me see that. You've helped me discover things about myself that have been hidden behind layers of fear and insecurity. You've *seen* me. And I see you."

A small smile finally broke through. He slowly lifted his hand and caressed the medal with his thumb. "I haven't looked at this in years. I shoved it in a drawer and tried to forget everything about the day that led to me receiving any sort of recognition. In my mind, I was responsible for death, not life. My choices led to damage and destruction, and nothing beyond that stuck with me."

The far-off look in his eyes told her he was back in that place—back to a time he tried so hard to forget. Maybe she'd made a mistake. Maybe she should have put the medal back in the drawer and not reminded him of everything he'd lost. "Sometimes we need to be reminded of the good we've done, but I'm sorry if I overstepped. I didn't mean to upset you."

His gaze focused on her, and he lifted his thumb to rest on her jawline. "All you've done is show me I can't outrun my past. That every decision led me to this moment. And you're right, the day good men died should be remembered and honored. I did everything I could to save them all and succeeded in saving some. I need to see the big picture and remember the good I did."

The tension tying up her insides vanished. She laid the medal down on the bed and leaned into his touch. "You're a good man. The best man. Don't ever forget that."

He grinned, a wicked gleam in his eyes. "I'm not that good."

Oh, dear Lord. Heat curled in her core. She bit her bottom lip, waiting for him to make a move. To say more. To do something to stop the burning desire growing inside her like a raging fire.

"It's late. I should let you get settled and sleep. It's been a long day."

Disappointment threatened to squelch that fire, but she wasn't ready for him to go. Wasn't ready to say goodbye and spend a night alone in the big bed. She wanted more. She wanted him.

"I don't want you to leave."

An almost pained expression flashed on his pinched face. He said nothing, only the sound of his heavy breathing in the room.

Maybe she'd been wrong. Maybe he didn't feel the same way about her as she did him, and his concern was only out of obligation. Maybe the roundness of her belly was too much for him—a reminder of her past he couldn't handle.

But now wasn't the time for hesitation and second-guessing. It was her time to finally take what she deserved.

"Cade, will you stay with me tonight?" She held his gaze, unwilling to look away even though fear of rejection threatened to take her out at the knees.

"Are you sure that's what you want?"

"More than anything."

He traced his thumb from her jawline to her mouth before dropping his hand to rest at her waist. Taking her mouth with his, he wrapped his arms around her then laid her down on the soft bed. She wasn't sure where the night would lead them, but there was no doubt it'd be one she'd remember forever.

CADE MOVED his hands along Laura's sides as his lips devoured her. His fingers itched to touch her silky skin. To lift the tank top and feel every inch of her body.

But he'd promised himself to take things slow. A couple of kisses were one thing. Crossing the line of intimacy while she was so vulnerable was another.

Breaking the kiss, he propped up his elbow and rested his head on his fist. He stared down at her, studying her swollen lips and the light blush on her cheeks. Her blond hair was fanned out against the white pillowcase. His heart climbed into his throat. She was so damn beautiful.

"Is something wrong?" she asked.

He shook his head and skimmed her cheek with his knuckles. "In this moment, everything is perfect."

He meant it to his bones. Nothing else mattered. All his troubles floated away. All he wanted was Laura, with him always.

She frowned, and he hated the uncertainty dancing in her

eyes. "Then why did you pull away? Is it because..." as her voice trailed off, she cradled her belly.

"Never. I just...I want to do this right. We've started this off in a pretty unconventional way."

She let out a small laugh. "Ya think?"

He grinned, glad to see some of her humor back. "I can't say I'm mad about that, because I'm not sure what else would have pushed me into finally confronting my feelings for you."

A sexy smirk lifted the corner of her mouth. "I'm not sure if I should be offended or flattered. It only took multiple attacks and a threat on my life for you to make a move."

"Flattered. Definitely." Chuckling, he kissed the smirk off her face. "I prefer to think of it as painfully keeping a respectful distance while trying not to kill your ex-boyfriend. Then there was your brother to think about. Hitting on his baby sister who is ten years younger might land me a punch in the gut and cost me a best friend."

Her face sobered. "It still might cost you those things. Matthew wasn't happy when he saw us together."

"True, but I can't live my life to make other people happy. Not anymore. Besides, something else is going on with him. I don't know if it has to do with the screwy things we've uncovered or not, but I don't like it."

"Me neither. He's always been so solid. The one person I can count on. Right now, it's like he's another person entirely. I don't understand why he won't confide in me or you or even Jude. But if he does take issue with us, will it bother you?"

"Your brother is my best friend in the world. He's helped me through some of the darkest moments in my life, and if he'll let me, I'll help him with whatever mess he's in. But regardless of how he feels about us, I want to be with you."

A slow, lazy smile took over her face. She glanced at him from under long, dark lashes. "Never in a million years did I think I'd hear those words from you. I always had the biggest crush on you. Once I got older, that crush threatened to grow but I stomped it down. Told myself it was a silly fantasy that needed to die with all my other dreams. Now I know I have a lifetime of dreams ahead of me."

He swept a strand of hair off her face then rested his forehead to hers. He breathed her in. Her scent was intoxicating. "You can have the damn world on a platter, and I'll help give it to you. But I want to do it right. Take it slow and get to know you on this different level. I don't want to rush in and ruin anything."

"I understand," she said, pulling away to sit. "If you don't want to stay in here with me, I get it. I really do. I just don't like the idea of being away from you. Even when I'm sleeping."

He gently guided her back down beside him and snuggled her close. She fit against him like a missing part of himself he never realized he needed. "Don't you dare move."

She rested a palm on his chest, swirling her fingers against his shirt. The slow, rhythmic motion sent pikes of lust shooting through his veins.

He gritted his teeth. How could such an innocent touch drive him so crazy? Trapping her hand against his chest with his own, he pressed his lips to her temple. "Can we stay like this tonight? Just be together?"

"I'd love that."

So he gathered her in his arms and held her close, listening to the gentle beat of her heart until he finally fell asleep.

19

W arm, fuzzy tingles of excitement continued to erupt inside Laura all the way into town the next morning. The night before had been filled with kisses she'd hoped would go a bit further and tender touches on the cusp of something more. Talks of the future that fell just short of promises.

She'd have given her right arm to stay curled up in bed with him all day, but that wasn't an option. Not with everything else going on beyond the safe walls of Cade's home.

Cade parked his truck in Mrs. Collins' driveway. He lifted Laura's hand and kissed her knuckles. "Mrs. Collins wants to talk specifics about a possible shelter. Then we can figure out any changes she may want to make regarding the original plans for the pantry."

"I'll try not to put pressure on her," Laura said and unfastened her seatbelt.

"Not sure you need to. She was pretty excited about your vision. And you're right, not much needs done to transform the house into a shelter. The biggest expenses will probably be furniture to turn the extra space into bedrooms and living quarters."

Before she could respond, he jumped out of the truck and hurried around to open her door. She grinned as he took her hand and helped her down, linking their fingers on their way up the sidewalk to the front door.

The mid-morning sky was filled with white fluffy clouds. School-aged kids played in nearby lawns, their giggles joining with the chirping robins. Joy radiated inside her warmer than the mid-morning sun.

She couldn't wait to hear the sweet giggles from her own baby. To see first smiles and watch first steps. To witness milestones as the years flew by. And for the first time since she'd found out she was pregnant, she could see a partner by her side, helping her raise that child with love and respect.

Cade's gentle touch on the small of her back guided her up the stairs to the large wrap around porch and to the front door. He knocked, keeping her close as they waited for Mrs. Collins to answer.

"After we're done here, what's next?" she asked. A part of her wanted to suggest putting a pause on all the problems surrounding them.

"I'm not sure. We can figure it out later. I want to see how you're feeling before we make any more plans for the day. You've had so much stress. That can't be good for the baby."

"Says the man who has a concussion." She rolled her eyes playfully before turning more serious. "How's your head?"

"Not too bad." He knocked again and frowned. "That's strange. She's usually at the door before we're out of the truck."

"True, but she's also always bustling around the property. She may have forgotten the time. Could be out back tackling the weeds or upstairs and didn't hear you knock. Did you check to see if the door's locked? I'm sure she wouldn't mind if we let ourselves in."

Small towns were filled with folks who didn't lock up at night—or at all, really. Mrs. Collins usually kept her home open to anyone in need, so stepping inside without her there to welcome them wouldn't be a huge intrusion.

He knocked one more time, then pressed the bell. After a few seconds, he tested the handle. The door swung open. He glanced over his shoulder at her, eyebrow cocked.

She bypassed him and stepped inside. "Mrs. Collins?" she called out.

No response.

"Maybe you were right and she's upstairs or outside," Cade said. "Just in case, stay close while we look."

His suggestion burst the bubble of happiness she'd been inside all morning. "Do you think something happened to her?"

He ran a palm up and down her arm. "I'm sure she's fine, but I don't want to take any risks. Let's check the backyard first."

Setting her purse on the side table, she stayed close to his back as they moved from the foyer through the kitchen to the back door. A quick glance outside showed nothing but overgrown grass and weeds Mrs. Collins had been combatting. A carriage house with rusted siding and broken shingles sat in the far corner of the lawn.

"Doesn't look like she's outside. Let's try upstairs." She struggled to keep her voice from shaking. There was no reason to think there was anything wrong with Mrs. Collins. But the pit in her stomach grew by the second.

Cade ducked his head in each of the rooms on the first floor before bounding up the stairs.

She trailed behind him. The baby inside her swollen belly insisted on pressing on her lungs, making each step harder than normal. Taking a second, she rested her fingers along the smooth banister and sucked in a deep breath.

A tiny flutter stirred inside her. She stilled, roaming her

palm over her stomach in search of where the sensation started.

Another flutter, like the flap of butterfly wings, moved her hand to her side. Movement against her touch confirmed what she'd felt, and her heart tripled in size.

The baby was kicking.

Grinning, she started back up the steps. She wanted Cade to experience this moment with her. She'd felt the baby move before, but he hadn't. She wanted him to be a part of these special moments from the beginning.

"Laura! Call 911. Now!"

Cade's gruff command wiped out all her excitement and filled her with dread. She patted her pockets, searching for her phone, as she hurried to the top of the stairs. She spotted Cade hunched over Mrs. Collins, who laid curled in a ball at the base of the stairs leading up to the third floor.

Her eyes were closed. Her skin pale. Blood pooled beneath her head, staining the wooden floors.

Bile sloshed in her stomach, chasing away the wonderful feel of her baby from moments before. "Oh my God. Is she alive?"

"She has a pulse. She's needs to get to the hospital quick. There's only so much my emergency medical training can do."

"Crap. My phone's in my bag downstairs." She turned to run down the steps, careful with her footing as she made her way back to the foyer.

Heavy footsteps turned her toward the kitchen. Isaac stood with a grin on his scruffy face and a gun aimed at her head. "Hello, darling. Glad to see you finally showed up. Now keep your mouth shut and head out the back before you force me to do something I'll regret."

~

CADE'S PULSE raced like a freight train. It'd been years since he'd had to call upon the limited medical training he'd received in the military. A wave of heat slammed against him as anxiety swelled in his gut. Beads of sweat dotted his hairline.

Okay. Deep Breaths. One step at a time.

He pressed his index and ring fingers to the thin skin at her neck again. Her pulse was as weak and thready as it'd been the first time he'd checked. The blood leaking from the gash on the side of her head was alarming, but also wasn't surprising for a head wound.

The most critical issue was how long ago she'd fallen. How long had she laid there unconscious?

Time ticked by. He strained his ears for signs of Laura but didn't hear anything. "Laura," he called out. "Is an ambulance on the way?"

Nothing.

"Laura!"

More silence.

Shit. He couldn't take a chance that Laura hadn't made the call for help yet. He grabbed his phone and called 911.

"911, what's your emergency?" The woman on the other end of the phone spoke in a calm, no-nonsense tone.

"I have an older woman who appears to have fallen down the stairs. Her pulse is weak. A wound to the side of the head has produced a substantial amount of blood. No idea how long ago she fell. I need an ambulance at 725 Grand Pine Road."

"Sending help now."

Mrs. Collins stirred slightly and moaned.

A beat of relief pulsed through him. "She's waking a bit," he told the dispatcher.

"Tell her not to move," the dispatcher said.

He placed a hand on Mrs. Collins' shoulder. "Stay still. You're going to be okay. It's Cade and Laura. We're getting help for you."

Her eyes fluttered open. Her pupils were huge, face pinched in pain. She squirmed on the floor, causing another moan to rumble from her chest. She opened her mouth as if trying to say something, but nothing came out.

"Shh, everything's going to be okay." He prayed that was true. Sirens sounded in the distance. "It won't be long now until help's here."

She latched her gaze on his and clung onto his arm with more strength than he'd think possible. "Pushed."

The word came out on a whisper. He leaned closer. "What did you say?"

"Didn't fall. Was pushed." As if speaking was too much to handle, her eyes drifted closed again and her body went lax.

Terror clamped onto the back of his neck with icy fingers. *Laura!*

"Mrs. Collins, I have to go check on Laura. I'll be right back. You aren't alone, okay. Help's on the way." He hated leaving the older woman, but he jumped to his feet and ran down the stairs. He still had the dispatcher on the line, so he pressed the phone to his ear. "She woke for a second. Said she was pushed. Send police."

Without waiting for a response, he disconnected the call and dialed Laura. He reached the first floor and swung into the foyer. A ringing phone greeted him. Laura's bag sat on the side table where she'd left it, her phone obviously inside, but she was nowhere to be seen. He disconnected and shoved his device in his pocket.

"Laura?" he yelled, praying for her to prove him wrong and walk down the hall. But she never appeared.

He ran into the kitchen, heart pounding. She wasn't there, but the back door stood ajar.

They hadn't opened the door when they'd searched for Mrs. Collins, which meant someone had recently used it.

Isaac.

Anger turned his blood hot, and he sprinted out the door, spinning in a circle to see every single inch of space around him. "Laura!" He screamed her name, willing her to appear.

Shit. Shit. Shit.

The sirens grew louder, closer, and he ran back inside. Each footstep echoed the panic tightening his chest. Two medics made it to the front door carrying a stretcher along with a medical bag as a deputy cruiser pulled into the driveway.

"The victim's at the base of the stairs on the second floor," he yelled as he passed them. He wanted Mrs. Collins to be okay, but right now, he had an even bigger problem. One he needed Deputy Owen Wells for.

Frowning, Owen stepped out of his cruiser. "What happened?"

"Laura's missing. I swear, if Isaac has her, I'll kill the sonofabitch."

Owen held up his palms. "Slow down. First, threatening to kill someone in front of a sheriff's deputy isn't the best decision. Second, I thought I was here because a woman was pushed down the stairs. I need you to start from the beginning."

Cade shoved a hand through his hair. He didn't have time to go through everything from the freaking beginning. His gut told him Laura was in trouble and time was running out. As quickly as he could, he recapped what had happened for Owen.

Owen gave one, brief nod and worked his jaw back and forth. "Any idea who pushed Mrs. Collins?"

He gave a derisive snort. "Is there any question? It has to be Isaac. Dammit, we're wasting time. We have to find Laura. She wouldn't just disappear. Especially when she left my side to call for help."

Commotion turned him back to the front of the house. The medics carried Mrs. Collins on the stretcher and hurried toward the ambulance.

Owen pushed the button on the side of the communicator attached to his shoulder as he moved toward the medics. "I need a few uniforms at 725 Grand Pine Road. Missing woman in potential danger. Need to locate Laura Metcalf, blond hair. Blue eyes. Five foot, two inches. Suspected to be with Isaac Heck."

Cade followed, his pace clipped. Each sentence pierced him like a knife. Police shouldn't need to be called. Laura shouldn't be missing. If he'd done his job, none of this would be happening. Laura would be beside him. Not gone with a man who'd hurt her time and time again.

But this time would be different. He'd move mountains to bring her home. And when he did, he'd never let anyone hurt her. Never let anyone take her away from him again. He'd love her every damn day like she deserved to be loved.

But first, he had to find her.

20

Cade watched helplessly as the ambulance disappeared down the street. Owen barked orders to deputies, who fanned out in search of clues to Laura's whereabouts. All the chaos and terror created a buzz in his brain. A fog that settled over him, making his vision grainy and sounds of the day distant.

The sun still shone bright, the clouds fluffy and white like they'd been drawn by a child. Everything should be right—should be perfect on a day like this.

But things were far from perfect. Everything was wrong. Very, very wrong.

The ringing phone in his pocket pulled Cade from the dark pit of panic assaulting him with every worst-case scenario. A beat of hope made his pulse race as he answered the phone. "Hello? Laura? Is that you?"

"Hi, Cade. It's Brooke. Is everything okay?"

The concern leaking through the speaker shook his senses, and he lowered himself onto the porch steps. Dammit, he needed to get a grip. He wouldn't do Laura a lick of good by falling apart. She needed him now more than ever. "Laura's missing. Police are searching for her."

"What? Where are you? What happened?"

He pinched the bridge of his nose as he tried to put his frantic thoughts together. "We stopped by the food pantry. Mrs. Collins was hurt, and while trying to get help, Laura went missing. The back door was open. I know Isaac has her. He pushed an old woman down the stairs and waited until we got here so he could grab her."

"Are you sure it's Isaac? There's no one else it could be? Sometimes if we make up our minds before we have all the facts, we miss things right in front of our faces."

Frustration tightened his grip on the phone. He'd heard rumblings around town about what had happened to Brooke and her now-husband Lincoln, but this was different. His gut told him Isaac had finally gotten his hands on Laura.

He hadn't trusted his instincts in the past. He wouldn't make that mistake again.

"I know who has her. I just need to figure out where." Determination strengthened his resolve. They hadn't vanished into thin air. The police had been searching for Isaac's whereabouts since yesterday and came up short, but they had to be missing something.

"I want to help. Anything I can do, any resources I can bring, you've got it."

"Thanks. I appreciate that. But right now, I don't even know where to start."

"I'm going to call Jude, and we'll meet you. Three heads are better than one, and Jude might have more ideas of where Isaac might go. The other stuff can wait."

"What other stuff?" he asked, frowning.

"Why I called. I found the payment information you wanted. But that's not important right now. We can talk about it later."

He sighed, not really caring but needing to know what Brooke had found. "It's fine. Really. Tell me."

"Okay. Well, I pulled up my banking information. I noticed a difference with who the checks were made out to. The larger amount, the one that matches the estimate you and Matthew gave me, was written to Mountaintop Construction. The other check, the one matching the amount needed to pay the extra cost not covered by the Community Outreach Foundation, was written to Mountaintop Construction Co. A subtle difference, but a difference nonetheless."

He rubbed at his forehead. The pain throbbing against his skull had less to do with his concussion and more to do with the constant turmoil boiling inside him. He tried to understand the importance of the information Brooke gave him but came up empty. "Wouldn't both of those checks still be deposited into the same account?"

"Not necessarily," Brooke said, drawing out words. "If there are two different accounts, each with different names on them, they'd go to different places. You might assume adding Co. at the end of the company name wouldn't be a big deal, but if paperwork is drawn up at a bank to indicate that specific difference, then each would be given a different account number. So the checks would end up deposited in two different places."

"Shit." One more thing to add to the pile. "I need to find out whose name is on that account. But honestly, I can't bring myself to care about that right now. None of it matters. All that matters is finding Laura."

A beat of silence lingered on the phoneline before Brooke responded. "I agree that Laura's the priority, but the police are searching at the logical places for her and for Isaac. We need to think outside the box. Follow the clues from a different angle. This might be that angle."

"How?" he asked, his voice cracking. No matter how he played it all in his mind, he couldn't see a connection between Isaac kidnapping Laura and the possible embezzlement using the community fund as a front. None of it made any sense.

"You ever hear the expression coincidences are bullshit?"

He snorted. "Not exactly in those terms."

"Well, as a cop, that's how we said it. Until we can think of another plan, let's follow this trail and see where we end up. It might surprise you."

He wanted to say no. He wanted to run from door to door and demand answers, ask questions. But Owen had already orchestrated a search party who was doing those exact things. Sheriff's deputies and city police were tracking leads and combing the area for any place Isaac could have taken her—had ABP's out for his vehicle since yesterday. As much as he wished he could be in the mix, he wasn't a cop, and he didn't have the same resources they had to find Laura.

Brooke was right. She was smart and capable, not to mention had experience as an officer. If she thought pulling on this string could help unravel the mystery, he'd yank as hard as he could on the damn thing.

"Meet me at my office. I'll text Matthew and tell him what happened. No matter what else he has going on, that should get his ass there."

Having a plan, even if he didn't understand how it could help, took away the hard edges of helplessness. He disconnected and pounded out a text to Matthew.

Laura's missing. Come to the office now.

He stared at the three little dots that appeared on the screen below his message, waiting for a response to pop up.

But none came.

Pushing to his feet, he stalked over to Owen. "Any news?"

Owen shook his head. "Afraid not. We've called in all the help we can. We already had an officer staked out at Isaac's house in case he showed up, which he never did, and his vehicle was found abandoned in a parking lot outside of town last night."

"Does he have any other properties or vehicles registered to his name?"

"None. We're doing everything within our power to find Laura. I promise."

"Call me if you hear anything," he said. Cade blew out a long breath. Tension bunched up his muscles. Nervous energy zipped through his body, and he fisted and unfisted his hands. He stormed to his truck. He needed answers and nothing would stop him from finding them.

A DESPERATE NEED TO figure out the world's most frustrating—and dangerous—puzzle forced Cade to rummage through everything he could find in Matthew's office. One by one he pulled papers from the filing cabinet then discarded them on the floor when nothing useful was found.

Fuck.

If there was something worth finding, he'd get his hands on it before the day was done. Privacy be damned.

"Cade?" Jude's voice cracked, and she ran into the room, throwing herself into his arms as sobs shook her body. "We have to find her. Isaac is a ticking time bomb. There's no telling what he'll do to her this time."

Wade, Jude's fiancé, and Brooke followed in behind her.

Cade squeezed Jude like a lifeline. "I'm so sorry. I shouldn't have let her leave my side. I should have kept her with me."

Jude pulled back and wiped away her tears with the heels of her hands. "From what I've heard, you were trying to help Mrs. Collins. There was no way of knowing the whole thing was orchestrated."

"Have you spoken with Matthew?" Wade asked. His usual

jovial expression was replaced with a furrowed brow and angry eyes.

Wade understood what it was like to have the woman you loved missing and in danger. He'd gotten Jude back, and Cade had to believe the same would be true of Laura. Because if he didn't believe that with his entire being, he'd crumble on the spot.

"No." Cade swallowed the bitter disappointment of not being able to reach Matthew. "I sent a text, called, and left a voicemail and nothing. I know he's going through something, but I can't stomach the idea he has any involvement with Laura's disappearance."

Jude shook her head. "Never. It has to be Isaac."

Brooke cleared her throat, drawing all eyes her way. "I understand the fear and even the assumption, but like I said before, we need to keep our minds as open as possible."

Cade wouldn't argue, but the look he shared with Jude told him they both knew who'd taken Laura.

"What are you doing now?" Wade asked, gaze searching the mess piling up on the ground.

"Hell if I know." Cade hooked an arm on the open drawer of the filing cabinet and hung his head. "Hoping something—anything—will jump out at me. I called the bank and asked about the names on the account Brooke found, but they can't tell me a damn thing. I need paperwork or statements, something to point to a name."

"And you think you'll find them here?" Jude asked. "Why would Matthew even have a business account you couldn't access?"

The question caused the tension in his head to double. The last thing he wanted was to go through his and Laura's suspicions, but Jude and Wade had to be let in on the details if they'd be of use. He quickly hit the bullet points while flipping through more paperwork.

Jude wrinkled her nose. "So you think my brother is using your company to clean money he's stealing from the Community Outreach Foundation?"

"I don't know what I think anymore, and honestly, I don't care if he's stealing from every business in town. I just want to find any crumb that can lead me to Laura. Brooke was right. The police are looking at all the logical avenues. We need to come at this from a different angle, and right now, this is the only other angle we've got."

Wade rested a heavy hand on his shoulder and squeezed. "All right. We're here to help. Time's ticking, so Jude and I will look in the reception area while you and Brooke stay here. We'll keep trying to get ahold of Matthew, too."

"And my mom," Jude said. "She'll be beside herself with worry, and maybe she'll have some insight on Matthew. She doesn't say much, but she's always listening. Always watching. She may know more than she realizes."

Cade hadn't considered Nicole as a source of information. She was so tied to Jenson that he doubted she'd give away anything that would implicate or even piss off her husband.

Jude paused in the doorway, aiming sad, terrified eyes his way. "Have you run any of this by my dad?"

"No. He's a slippery sonofabitch. And as much as I can't stand him, he's smart. Smart enough to not tell me anything useful. If he's involved in this the way I think he is, then he already has an escape plan." A thought nagged at him, and he cringed at giving voice to it. "Would he help Isaac?"

Jude squeezed her eyes shut for a beat. "He'd do whatever he could to save his reputation. But right now, with the police hunting down Isaac, he'd want distance there. Isaac's a liability now, and Dad can take on the role of worried father who'd do anything to get his daughter back."

His stomach turned. Jenson was an opportunist. He'd use Laura's disappearance for his gain without a real care for her safety. But that wouldn't matter as long he could help bring her home.

When Jude disappeared down the hall, Brooke wheeled the chair away from the desk. Determination set her mouth in a firm line. "I'll search the desk."

He nodded, appreciating her willingness to dive in and do whatever needed done, then brought his attention back to the filing cabinet. His vision blurred as fear made his mind spin. Bile sloshed around his insides and his chest threatened to explode. His phone burned a hole in his pocket as he willed it to ring. Willed Owen to be on the other end of the line, notifying him they'd found Laura.

He glanced at file after file, but nothing showed him anything new. The pile on the floor grew as he tossed things behind him. No time to bother with keeping things clean or worrying about Matthew's feelings. Matthew's lack of involvement or concern only fueled his anger.

"Do you have a safe in here?" Brooke asked, breaking into his escalating thoughts.

Frowning, he whipped around. "A safe? I don't think so. Why?"

"Because I found a key." She lifted up a small silver key.

He crossed the room, studying the key. "I've never seen that before." He plucked it from her hand, turning it over in search for some clue as to what it would unlock.

Standing, Brooke wiped her hands on the thighs of her jean shorts then turned in a circle. She scanned the room with narrowed eyes. "If Matthew has a safe, it'd be in here. I doubt he'd hide it somewhere else in the building."

He followed her line of vision, but nothing popped out as a hiding spot for some secret safe. "How many freaking secrets is my best friend keeping from me?"

"None." Matthew's hard tone turned him toward the doorway. "Dude. What the actual fuck? My sister is missing and you're in here ransacking my office? For what? You should be out there trying to find her, or was everything you said about the two of you complete bullshit?"

The insult made the turmoil bubbling inside him boil over. He stormed over to Matthew and fisted the neck of his shirt in his hands, pushing into his personal space. "You have some nerve waltzing in here, questioning me. Questioning my motives. I'm in love with your sister and you don't even seem to care she's gone."

Matthew's eyes widened, his mouth fell open for a second before snapping shut. "I care. I care more than you'll ever know. She's my sister and she's in danger. I got here as soon as I got your messages. But I can't wrap my mind around what her being kidnapped has to do with you wrecking my office."

Jude placed a hand on Cade's shoulder, easing him back. "We need to stay calm."

Brooke cleared her throat, drawing everyone's attention. "Matthew, what's the key for?"

Scowling, Matthew stormed over to Brooke and snapped the key from her hand then turned toward a framed picture on the wall, revealing a wall safe behind it. He opened the safe, grabbed a handful of papers, then dropped them on the desk. "There."

Cade flipped through the papers. "What are these?"

"Information pertaining to the company." All the anger had left his voice, leaving Matthew sounding exhausted. "Tax papers, bank accounts, licenses, liability insurance. Everything I had to figure out when I was starting up the company. If you'll remember, we didn't know what the hell we were doing. You were still getting your feet under you. I handled all this shit. Honestly, if it wasn't for my dad helping me figure all this out, we wouldn't have ever gotten off the ground."

"Why hide it?" Cade asked, pissed about yet another aspect of his business he was unaware of.

Matthew snorted and lifted his hands before letting them fall to his side. "I was keeping it safe."

A bank statement caught his attention, and he unburied the rest of the paper. The name Mountaintop Construction Co. was at the top of the paper with two names underneath.

Jenson and Matthew Metcalf.

The names were like a punch in the gut. Matthew was full of lies, and for the first time, he'd been caught red handed.

21

The houses got farther apart, and the crowd of trees grew thicker the longer Laura was in the car—a car she'd never seen before. Isaac had either bought a new one or stolen this one. She didn't bother to ask which. He'd clearly gone over the deep end, and she wouldn't put any erratic behavior past him.

Which only cranked up the terror clawing inside her.

She kept her gaze fixed out the passenger window. He'd taken back roads out of town, and now they wound higher and higher up the mountain. She searched her memory for anything that looked familiar, but nothing came to mind.

So much for escaping him and finding help. She had no phone and no sign of civilization anywhere around. Unless she got lucky and stumbled on a hidden cabin tucked in the forest, there were almost as many dangers waiting for her in the woods as there were with Isaac.

Almost.

A quick glance in his direction showed he still had the gun in his lap, the barrel pointed in her direction. She could try to snatch it off his legs, but if she failed, she'd only ignite his anger further. Or cause an accident that could hurt the baby.

Think, think, think.

Isaac drove the sedan onto a dirt road, piquing her interest.

She straightened against the plush seat. Panic pitched high in her throat. She'd assumed since he hadn't killed her, he planned to keep her around. Maybe she'd been wrong. Maybe he just needed to take her somewhere off the beaten path before putting a bullet in her brain. "Where are we going?"

"Oh look, she speaks." He snorted then aimed a sneer in her direction. "I like it better when you keep your mouth shut."

"Too bad," she shot back. He may hold a ton of power, but she'd never let him control her again. Never be the submissive woman who held her tongue. She may be terrified of what was about to happen, but she wouldn't give him the satisfaction of seeing her fear.

He laughed. Not a snicker or chuckle, but a full belly laugh that pissed her off even more.

But he didn't answer her question.

The car bumped along the lane until it widened, and a small clearing opened up. A cabin sat in a patch of sunshine. Rounded stones made up the walls, trimmed in a deep brown. The lawn boasted colorful flowers and towering trees. If she wasn't trapped in a nightmare, the property could have been pulled from a fairytale.

But this was as far from a fairytale as she could possibly be.

Isaac parked the car at the front of the gravel drive. "We're going to go inside now, and you're not going to do anything stupid. You know I'm a good shot." He wiggled the gun in her face before stepping outside, eyes fixed on her through the window.

She pulled in a deep breath. He was right. He'd spent countless hours hunting with his grandfather growing up, and still snuck into the woods when he got a chance to take down a buck. Darting into the forest might sound tempting, but she'd be inviting more trouble. She needed a different plan, and hopefully there'd be enough time to formulate one.

A sharp knock on the passenger window jolted her back to the moment. Isaac stood by the door, the side of his mouth curved and brows raised. Unable to put it off any longer, she got out of the car. Her legs itched to run, to move, to get as far away from Isaac as possible. But she needed to be smart about every single decision she made.

Isaac scratched behind his ear. A softness fell over his features that made her more nervous than the sneer. "Listen. I didn't want to do things like this. Didn't want to escalate the situation more. I love you, and if you would have listened and come back home, I wouldn't have had to take things so far. To be so drastic. You forced my hand, and now we need to make the best of things."

Each word was like a slap in the face. "And how do you suppose we do that?"

"Well, keep an open mind. I tried really hard to do something special for you. For us. For our family."

She struggled not to let her jaw drop. Pushing an old woman down the steps, not caring if she lived or died, was making this special for her?

He grabbed hold of her arm and hauled her up the porch steps to the front door. His grin stayed in place as he swept her inside. The living room flowed into the kitchen, an island separating the two spaces. Not much furniture filled the house, but at least it was clean.

"I know it's not much now, at least not in here, but we can make it whatever we want. I haven't had time to furnish everything, but there's one room I really want you to see."

He forced her down the short hall, her stiff limbs making

her stride short and stilted. The scent of fresh paint assaulted her delicate senses and dread weighed her down.

Stopping in front of a closed door, he shifted to stand behind her and covered her eyes with his hands. The cold metal of the gun against her face sent shockwaves down her spine.

"Surprise," he said in a sing-song voice that skimmed the back of her neck, causing goosebumps to erupt up and down her arms.

He removed his hands and her stomach dropped to the old wooden floor.

"Go on," he said, pushing her forward. "Go inside and look."

A fresh coat of light blue paint was on the walls, and soft cream-colored carpet covered the floor. A crib took up the far wall with a matching changing table beside it. A rocking chair was nestled in the corner, holding a giant white teddy bear.

A lump of conflicting emotion lodged in her throat. Seeing all the baby furniture opened a flood of anticipation but knowing Isaac had placed it in this house—this place where he planned to keep her and the baby all to himself—filled her with so much terror and rage she could almost drown in it.

"Well, what do you think?"

She turned to look at him, needing to see if his excitement was genuine or an act. The dopey look on his face confirmed he was as delusional as she'd feared, which snapped something inside her. "I think you're crazy."

The backhand across her face came so quick it stole her breath. She took a step back and lifted her fingers to her burning cheek. Blood pooled in her mouth until she was forced to swallow it.

"I did this for you and that's what you say to me?" He screamed, spit flying from his mouth. "I love you, and I will have you. Forever. Don't you forget that."

Her body trembled as she struggled to find the right words to diffuse the situation. But nothing she said could make this better. Nothing would change him. The only way to survive was to get away from him, and fast.

A pounding on the door sent hope coursing through her veins. Had Cade found her?

A low growl rumbled from his chest. "Stay put and keep your mouth shut." He stormed out of the room.

She moved slowly toward the hall. Maybe there was a back door. She could get outside and run for the road, staying under the cover of the bushes and trees until she found help. The wooden floors creaked as she tiptoed from the room. Her body trembled with each step. She kept her ears tuned, listening for his return. Tears threatened to fall, but she held them back—held back the panic and fear gnawing her insides.

"What are you doing here?" Isaac barked out the question, even though his tone was a bit softer than before.

"I think I need to be the one asking questions."

The sound of her father's voice released a cry of relief. She'd never been so happy to hear her dad. He'd come for her, and Isaac would go behind bars where he belonged.

Crying, she ran toward the front of the house. "Dad! I'm here! I'm right here!"

Frowning, Jenson stepped inside and slammed the door closed. He spared her one, hard look before glancing at Isaac. "You really screwed shit up this time, son. Time to clean your mess."

CADE'S HEAD threatened to explode as he paced back and forth across the room. Discarded papers and files shuffled at his feet. Each step brought a new burst of anger, a gut-wrenching sense of betrayal.

Jude and Wade stayed silent and lingered by the doorway. Worry was bright in Jude's eyes, and she bit into her thumbnail, the movement making her look so much like Laura it stole his breath.

Brooke sat behind the desk, her mouth fixed in a small O as if trying to sort out all the information.

Matthew stared at the statement now clutched in his fist. "I don't get what you're so upset about. It's the paperwork I got from the bank when I opened the account."

Cade stopped and glared at his partner. "Are you kidding me? You can stop with the innocent act. I know what you and your father have been up to, and the fact that his name is on this account cements everything. What I can't wrap my head around is if one of you staged a break-in to get that stupid flash drive out of the reception desk, how could you hurt Laura? Throw her to the ground and risk harming the baby?"

The memory of Laura huddled, crying on the floor and cradling the child inside her crashed against him, finally pushing him past his breaking point. He marched across the room. He'd make Matthew pay for playing a part in hurting her —of having knowledge he hid that put a target on her back.

Jude rushed forward and put herself between him and her brother. "Wait a minute. Hold on and let's talk about this."

"Talk about what? How Matthew had a hand in Laura being tossed around like a rag doll? You could have killed her. Could have killed the baby."

"What the hell are you talking about?" Matthew screamed, pushing against the firm hand Jude had placed on his chest. "I would never hurt her. Never hurt a child." His voice cracked and tears sprang to his eyes. "Never a baby. All I want in this life is to have one of my own."

The raw pain in his voice stomped down Cade's anger. He shoved a hand through his hair. Yelling and hurling accusations wouldn't get them anywhere, and time was ticking. "I need you to explain everything to me. Starting with why your dad's name is on a bank account for our business—a bank account I knew nothing about—and ending with what the hell's been your problem the last couple days. As soon as shit started going down, you've been impossible to get ahold of. Acting cagey and erratic. I need answers and I need them now."

Matthew sniffed back tears, his face turning a pasty white. He shoved past Cade and ambled toward a vacant chair. He lowered himself in it and hung his head in his hands. "Dad helped me set things up. He talked to the bank, and I just signed whatever he put in front of me. I don't understand what that has to do with Laura going missing. But the break-in... Laura's attack.... I had nothing to do with that."

Suddenly exhausted, Cade shifted to lean against the wall. "Then where were you? You didn't tell me, Laura, or Jude."

Jude put a hand on Matthew's shoulder. "Let us in. We love you and want to help."

Matthew sighed and covered Jude's hand with his. "The day I left, Brandon and I got a call that the woman who was carrying our baby was going into labor. We needed to drop everything and get there right away."

Jude gasped and threw her arms around her brother. "Matthew! Why didn't you tell us? Congratulations."

"The baby didn't make it," he said, despair cracking his voice. "We've tried for years, wanted this for years. We've had adoptions fall through and waited for so long. So we got a surrogate and we didn't tell a soul. We didn't want to jinx it, but it didn't matter. The worst still happened."

It all made sense. Matthew leaving so abruptly. Not answering calls or being available. Acting distant and cold. Cade's heart shattered watching sobs shake his best friend shoulders. "Oh man. I'm so sorry." He wanted to say more. To give him something that would take away the pain, but nothing he said would make things better.

And he didn't want to be an insensitive dick, but they didn't have time to waste.

Matthew turned large, sad eyes his way. "I swear. I didn't even realize my dad's name was on the bank account. I opened that account so long ago, and he just walked me into the manager's office and told me where to sign. I didn't question him, didn't read through everything the way I should have."

"Did you know this account is under a different name than the one you and Cade give your clients?" Brooke asked quietly.

Matthew pulled away from Jude and frowned. "What do you mean?"

Crouching, Cade shuffled through the dumped files and found what he was looking for, handing it over to Matthew. "Look at the account name. This is the one where we deposit the checks we receive from clients. The other one your dad appears to be using to clean money he's stealing from the Community Outreach Foundation."

Matthew snatched the paper and compared it to the first one. "I don't understand. He's an asshole, but that community fund supports so many local projects. Does so much good for the town."

"And what better way to steal than through a foundation no one would question?" Cade asked. "It's all based on donations, and I'm sure no one at city hall is questioning your father's intentions with the funds. All he needed was a way to clean the money."

"I'm such an idiot. It all makes sense now." Matthew's voice sounded hollow, his face crumpled in the same way it had when he was a kid—filled with disappointment and anger.

Jude frowned. "What makes sense?"

"He was so eager to help," Matthew said with a small snort. "Wanted to show me the ropes and help get the business off the ground. Dad's never shown interest in me or my life. As much as I've always hated him, I've also wanted his approval. Seeing him fuss over what we were creating and having him beside me, guiding me..." he lifted his hands then let them fall. "I was right back to that excited boy who was finally getting his dad to say he's proud. And the whole time, he was just using me."

Something clicked for Cade, and he rounded the desk to get to Matthew's computer. "What's your password?" he asked, bringing the screen to life.

Matthew spit out the password.

Brooke moved the chair over to give him space. "What are you doing?"

"You're right. Your dad used you. He uses everyone, and always has." He clicked on the internet browser. "It's something he has in common with Isaac, and their relationship has always bugged the shit out of me. I even told Deputy Owens to ask your dad if he helped Isaac hide last night."

"You don't really think Jenson would help the man who threatened his daughter, do you?" Brooke asked.

Jude let out a light laugh filled with zero humor. "You have no clue the shit he's done."

Cade worked his jaw back and forth, hating Jenson Metcalf as much as he hated Isaac. "Police couldn't find any property Isaac owned and have no idea where he could be. But what if he doesn't own it? What if your dad does, or at least purchased it? What if he used you again?"

Matthew stood and came up behind him, bending to peer over his shoulder at the screen. "Is that the county auditor's website?"

Cade nodded and typed in Matthew's name.

"Why my name? You know everything Brandon and I own, and it's not much."

A new screen popped up, listing multiple properties under the name Matthew Metcalf.

"What the hell?" Matthew's voice pitched high, broadcasting his panic. "That's Brandon's and my home and the one underneath is the office building. I don't know what the third property is. Dude, I promise."

A beat of hope pushed its way through the fear eating Cade inside out. "Someone call Deputy Owen. We might have figured out where Isaac is holding Laura."

22

A bucket of icy water over her head couldn't have stunned Laura more. She darted her gaze between her father and Isaac, trying to wrap her mind around what was right in front of her eyes.

But she couldn't make it make sense.

"Daddy?" She barely recognized her own voice. It was so small, so quiet—like the little girl she used to be.

The little girl who'd held out hope for so long that her father would one day shower her with love.

Jenson didn't even bother to acknowledge her. "What the hell were you thinking? We had a plan. Now that plan has gone to shit."

"I know, I know. I'm sorry. She just.... pushed me into this decision. I didn't have a choice. And really, it's not that big of a deal."

She wanted to scream, to interject, to demand to know what was going on but she couldn't form the words. Couldn't assemble the myriad of thoughts jumbling her mind into actual sentences.

Jenson rolled his eyes. "Not a big deal? How do you figure?"

Isaac shrugged. "That old woman has to be dead, and there's no reason for anyone to suspect she was pushed. All I need is for Laura to tell everyone she found me because she wanted our family back together. Everything else is a big misunderstanding."

Her jaw dropped. Did he honestly think she'd just willingly go along with his plan? Pure, hot rage pooled in her core. She crossed her arms over her chest. "Forget it. I'll never cover for you. I'll never be with you."

Isaac swiveled and pointed the gun at her. "You'll do what I tell you, bitch."

Jenson blew out a frustrated breath. He marched to Isaac and lowered his arm so the gun was aimed at the floor. "How many times do I have to tell you to watch your temper? You lose your patience and make stupid decisions. That's why we're in this spot now, on the brink of ruining everything we've worked so hard to put in place."

Isaac deflated. "You're right. I'm sorry."

"Well, you should be," Jenson snapped. "She's obviously going to make this difficult, and police are combing the streets looking for her. Not to mention I've heard rumblings about Mrs. Collins waking briefly to tell that meddling jackass she was pushed. Didn't take much to put things together."

A sliver of hope shined through the deepening despair of Laura's situation. If Mrs. Collins told Cade what happened, the search for her would have started sooner than she thought. And waking at all had to be good news for Mrs. Collins.

"Shit," Isaac said, grounding the heel of his hand against the side of his head.

"Yeah. Shit is right. You need to take the cash we drained from the account and get the hell out of town. It's the only way for you now."

"What account?" Laura asked, unable to stop herself.

Her father shot a glare her way. "Stay out of it. You've caused enough trouble."

"I can't leave her and our baby," Isaac said, cutting back into the conversation. "I won't leave her. She's mine."

Jenson rested a hand on his shoulder. "She'll never listen. Not anymore. You know what you need to do."

"What does that mean?" she asked, her words shaking. "You'd let him kill me?"

Icy silence was his only response as he kept his focus latched on Isaac.

Terror and shock turned her stomach. Her father had always been a monster, but no way she'd ever imagined he was so vile. That he'd give the order to her executioner. "You can't mean it. You can't really be okay with him killing me. Killing your grandchild."

Jenson shrugged. "You've forced my hand." The sound of an approaching car stopped any more heinous words. He stormed toward the window and peeked past the curtains blocking the front yard from view. "You've got to be kidding me. Isaac, get Laura out of here and keep her quiet."

Isaac stormed toward her and grabbed her arm, yanking her back down the hall.

Alarm dug her heels into the floor. "I'm not going with you. You can shoot me right here."

"Dammit, Laura," Jenson sneered. "Go. Now."

"Why?" she asked, adrenaline causing a surge of strength she'd never felt before. "So you don't have to watch your daughter be murdered?"

A vein ticked along the long column of his throat. "Laura," he drew out her name like he had when she'd been a child, doling out threats and demanding obedience.

She lifted her chin, locking her narrowed gaze with her father.

Isaac jammed the gun against her throat. "Move!"

Her body tensed, preparing for the moment of pain before her life leaked from her body. She closed her eyes and rested a hand on her belly.

Sorry I couldn't protect you, little one. Mommy loves you.

The sound of the door swinging open and her father's muttered curses opened her eyes. Her mother stood in the doorway, a gun in her hands and devastation contorting her face in a way Laura had never seen.

"What the hell?" Isaac yelped.

The cool feel of metal left her skin as Isaac pivoted to face Nicole. This was her chance. She jammed her elbow into his gut and stomped hard on his foot.

"Oof." He released his grip and stumbled backward.

A gun went off, the sound vibrating her body and stealing her senses. She stilled, waiting for the explosion of the bullet to take her down, but nothing happened.

She chanced a quick glance over her shoulder. Isaac laid on the ground, blood pouring from some unseen wound.

"Run!" her mother screamed.

Laura took off as fast as she could toward the open door.

Nicole pointed her weapon at Jenson, who charged forward and grabbed her wrist. He twisted her arm. Her mom yelped.

Laura hesitated. She wanted to help her mom but if she stayed, she had no doubt her father would kill her.

"Get out of here!" Nicole yelled, as if sensing Laura needed the extra push to leave her behind.

She shimmied past her wrestling parents, blocking the grunts and cries. Tears stung her eyes and her heart threatened to crack in two, but she couldn't think about what was behind her. She had to focus on getting far away, saving herself and her unborn child.

Stumbling off the porch, she darted toward her mom's car. If she could get help fast enough, maybe she could help her mom. Get her away from her father.

Bang!

Her heart shot to her throat, but she couldn't turn around to see what happened. She needed to keep running. Keep moving forward.

"Enough, Laura!" Her dad yelled, stepping outside. "Look at all the trouble you've caused. At what you made me do. It's time for you to suffer the consequences of your actions. So be a good girl and get back in the house."

Slowly, she faced him. Twenty feet separated them. She shook her head, disgusted by the man in front of her. "No."

Then she turned away from her father and dove for the cover of her mom's car, reaching the other side seconds before a bullet ripped into the metal...inches above her head.

TREES WHIRLED by in a haze as Cade drove at breakneck speed up the mountain. Adrenaline zipped through his veins, mixing with the terror and rage simmering in the pit of his stomach. A slight tremor shook his hands, and he tightened his grip on the wheel to steady his nerves. He'd called Owen and let him know what they suspected, and the deputy had promised to check the house out himself.

But Cade refused to sit idly by and do nothing.

Brooke sat in the passenger seat, face set in fierce determination. She's insisted on coming with him, stopping at her truck to grab guns she'd brought from home. Jude and Wade had stayed behind, wanting to contact Nicole and see if she had any information that could be helpful—just in case the property they'd found was another dead end.

His phone rang through the speakers. The number that flashed on the in-dash screen was unknown, and a pulse of anticipation thumped along his veins. He pressed the button on the steering wheel to answer the call. "Hello?"

"Where are you?"

He tightened his jaw at Owen's gruff voice. "Have you found her?"

"I'm on my way to the location you gave me. Now, answer my questions. Where are you?"

He hesitated a second. He might not know Deputy Wells very well, but there was no doubt the other man wouldn't be happy. "On my way to the house we found."

"I thought I asked you to stay in town."

He snorted. "And I thought I told you I couldn't sit around twiddling my thumbs, waiting to hear news."

An exasperated sigh shook the speakers. "You charging in to save the day could put Laura in more danger. Drive around, clear your head, then go back to town and wait for me to call. I appreciate your help but let me take it from here."

He tore his gaze from the road for a quick second to glance at Brooke. Her hooked brows told him she'd follow his lead. She had experience with dangerous situations and understood how to handle a criminal, and he'd been through horrific shit overseas. The two of them weren't inexperienced civilians who'd make the situation worse.

"Sorry, man. Brooke and I are almost there. I'll only act if needed. We'll be careful."

He disconnected the call and blew out a long breath. He couldn't have Owen's words of doubt and discouragement make him second guess himself right now. He needed his head on straight—to trust his instincts and be prepared for anything.

"You sure you're ready for whatever we may find?"

He nodded, her solemn tone twisting his insides.

"Okay, so let's plan this out. Best case scenario, we knock on the door, Isaac answers, and we get Laura out. The chances of that happening are about zero percent. It's more likely, even if they're inside, no one will answer. But if he does, he'll be armed and ready to take out anyone who tries to stop him."

Cade's GPS announced an upcoming turn, and he slowed before leaving the back road for the narrow tree-lined lane. If he wasn't following directions, he'd think he was going straight into the forest. His heartrate increased with every bounce and jostle of his truck.

"I agree. If they're here, and he so much as hears us coming, he'll react. I'll park between some trees, and we go in on foot. The images I pulled up of the house show two entrances—one in the front and another through a back door that leads into the kitchen. Sneaking in through the back is our best bet."

Brooke nodded. "From there, we stay together. Go from room to room and keep our weapons ready. If we sense a threat to Laura or it's not smart for us to enter the home, we call Owen and share what we've found."

A clearing opened up, and Cade maneuvered the truck off the lane and wedged it between two large trees. He wanted to argue that he'd go in that house no matter what, but Brook was right.

Bang!

Panic set all his nerves to high alert. He steeled his mind against a hundred images of what might have happened—images of the horrific things he'd witnessed in the past—and charged out of the truck. The surprise of seeing several vehicles lining the driveway slowed his progress. Were they at the right place, or had they just stumbled upon another shit show?

A booming laugh turned him toward the front of the cabin. Jenson Metcalf stood on the porch, a gun in his hands pointed at a two-door sedan parked near the house. "Your boyfriend's here. Too bad he's too late." He unloaded another shot, the bullet colliding with the driver's side mirror.

The sound of Laura's scream set Cade's nerves on edge. His body tensed for a beat before he raised his own weapon at Jenson. He wasn't too late, but things could go south very quickly. "Give it up, Jenson. There's no way to talk your way out of this one. Sheriff's deputies are on their way here right now. Don't make things worse for yourself than they need to be."

Jenson finally glanced his way, but kept his handgun trained on the spot where Laura had taken cover. "I haven't done anything wrong. I came here looking for my daughter and found everyone dead. No one will question the word of a grieving father and husband."

"Mom," Laura cried. "He shot my mom."

Her cries were like a cleaver to the chest, but he had to keep his focus on Jenson. A flash of motion caught the corner of his eye—Brooke. He couldn't let anyone know she was there. If she could approach the side of the house without being noticed, she could disarm Jenson.

Cade took a step forward, making sure Jenson's sights were set straight on him. "Won't work. We already know too much. We know you stole money from the community fund and used Matthew's name to buy this property. Even if you weren't going down for whatever the hell this is, you'd be charged for embezzlement and money laundering."

Jenson's eyes grew wide. "All I did was help my son and this town. Anything Matthew did on his own...well that's on him."

Taking another step, he mentally calculated the distance between him and Laura's father. Close to a hundred feet separated them. He'd need to close the distance by at least half if he stood a chance at taking him down.

"Don't move another inch," Jenson warned. "Trust me. This isn't how I wanted things to end. But when people don't listen to me, I have to take matters into my own hands."

His calm and steady tone almost activated Cade's gag reflex. How could a father choose to gun down his own daughter?

"Let Laura go," Cade said. "You know you don't want to hurt her."

Jenson laughed again, then jumped off the porch, closing the space between him and the car.

Cade took off at a dead sprint. Sweat trickled down his spine. His heart thundered in his ears. He couldn't lose Laura. Not like this. Not after everything they'd been through. He loved her, and he'd never even gotten a chance to tell her.

"Stop right there before I put a bullet in your back." Brooke emerged from woods, weapon aimed at Jenson. "Drop your weapon and put your hands in the air."

Jenson stopped but he aimed once more at the car.

Brooke squeezed the trigger, the blast deafening.

Jenson fell to the ground, the gun dropping on the gravel drive. "Sonofabitch," he yelled through gritted teeth.

Cade hurried to Jenson and kicked the gun far from his reach as Brooke removed a pair of handcuffs and slapped them on his wrists.

"Laura," Cade yelled, rounding the vehicle. "It's over, baby. You're safe."

She sat on the ground with her hands over her ears. Tears ran down her dirty face, and her hair fell in a tangled curtain around her shoulders. Her bottom lip trembled, and she stared up at him with large, terrified eyes.

He dropped to his knees and pulled her into his arms. "Are you hurt? Did he touch you?"

Shaking her head, she clung to him. "My mom. He hurt her. She needs help."

The faint call of sirens interrupted her words.

"Hear that? Help's coming." He supported her weight as he guided her to her feet, an arm remaining tight around her waist. "I can't believe we found you. I was so damn scared. I love you, Laura. I love you so much."

She offered a small smile and threw her arms around his neck. "I lov—"

"You bitch!" Isaac screamed and tore from the house like a madman. Blood stained his white shirt. He pressed one hand against his side and trained his gun at the back of

Laura's head with the other. "I told you, you're mine forever."

Cade spun as fast as he could, placing himself between Laura and the blast that erupted milliseconds later. Pain shot through him in giant waves before his body went numb.

Another shot exploded into the air followed by the sounds of Isaac's cries of pain.

"Stay down, you asshole!" Brooke yelled. "You're not getting away this time."

Cade collapsed onto the hard stones. Darkness edged out his vision. The soft touch of warm hands on his face and the sound of his name made him smile.

"Laura?" He squinted. Her beautiful face came into view. Her pouty lips, the soft curve of her chin, the delicate slope of her nose. "So pretty. So special. You're my everything."

"Open your eyes, Cade. Look at me, honey. Stay with me."

He tried. Tried so hard to do what she asked. He hated when she cried—hated her being upset about anything. All he wanted was for her to be happy.

"Please. Please, Cade. Don't leave me. Don't leave us."

Someone lifted his hands and he felt the hard bump on her stomach. The child inside her was safe and that's all the mattered. He'd shown them love while he could. Shown them they could have any future they wanted.

Wishing he could have been a part of their lives for just a little while longer, his eyes grew heavy, and the world went black.

23

The steady beep of the machines in the hospital room combined with the florescent lights and strained nerves, keeping Laura wide awake despite the late hour.

Well, that and the uncomfortable chair she'd dragged beside Cade's bed.

She hadn't left his side since his surgery to remove the bullet lodged into his back. Doctor Simon had told the group of family and friends gathered in the waiting room he'd been lucky. The bullet had missed all his vital organs and been removed without incident.

But he'd yet to wake up.

"Hey, you," Jude said, stepping into the room beside Matthew. "How are you holding up?"

Laura shrugged and sniffed back the tears threatening to fall. The day had been long and filled with stress and fear, but she only wanted to put positive energy in the room. She'd do anything to see Cade open his eyes. To fit under his arm, attack him with kisses, and tell him how she loved him.

Matthew dragged over two more chairs, one on each side of

Laura, and sat. He rested a hand on her knee. "He's strong. He'll wake soon. He's always been a little lazy. Likes his sleep too much."

His light teasing coaxed a small smile from her. "He just needs some time. How's Mom?"

Brooke had leapt into action and taken Isaac down as soon as he'd fired the shot that had hit Cade. Everything that followed was a bit of a blur. Sheriff deputies, local police, and EMT's had swarmed the property. Her mother and father were transported to the local hospital, but she'd ridden with Cade.

She'd kept up to date on her mother's condition, but nothing could pry her from Cade's side.

"She woke for a few minutes and asked about you," Jude said, squeezing Laura's hand. "We told her you were all right and with Cade. She fell back asleep before we left the room. She's going to be okay."

"She found me. She helped me get out of that house." Emotion lodged in her throat as flashbacks of seeing her mom, of hearing the gunshot, shook her senses. "She finally stood up to Dad—tried to protect me. I thought he killed her."

The tears fell. How many times had she hoped her mom could break the chains of abuse and intervene? Could be brave enough to support her children the way they truly needed?

Nicole had finally taken that step and it'd almost cost her life.

Matthew hooked an arm around her shoulder and pulled her close. "He might have tried, but she's stronger than any of us gave her credit. She'll pull through, and he's already in a jail cell. Right beside that good for nothing ex of yours. Where they'll both stay for a very long time."

She breathed in her brother's familiar scent of cedar and peppermint. He'd been her rock so many times. Having him by her side, by Cade's side, turned her insides to mush. "I still can't believe Dad was going to just let him kill me."

Matthew pressed a kiss to her temple. "He can't hurt you anymore. He can't hurt any of us, and it looks like you have one hell of a protector willing to do anything to keep you safe."

She stared at Cade's closed eyes. His breathing was slow and even, and a light color touched his cheeks under his scruff. "He has to be okay."

"He will be."

The catch in Matthew's voice reminded her of what Jude had told her about why he'd been acting so strangely the last few days. "I'm sorry about the baby." She rested a hand on her belly, the reminder that this life inside her was so fragile tightening her chest. "I'm sure seeing me like this is hard. I get why you kept your distance."

"Hey, now," he said, topping her hand with his. "My distance had nothing to do with you and everything to do with needing some time to process and grieve. I take my uncle duties very seriously and will love this child so damn much."

"Not as much as Aunt Jude, though." Jude placed her palm on top of Matthew's.

Despite the fear still churning in her gut, a peace and happiness settled over her like she hadn't known in years. She had her brother and her sister beside her, no matter what the future held.

"You two will have to get in line. No one will love that baby more than me." Cade's dry voice was so weak it barely registered in Laura's ears.

A sharp gasp stirred in her throat, and she scooted to the edge of her seat. "Cade?"

He stared back at her and grinned.

Matthew stood then dragged Jude from her chair. "We'll give you two some privacy. Good to see you awake, man. You gave us all quite a scare. Thank you for saving her."

Cade dipped his chin.

Laura waited for her siblings to leave before wedging Cade's hand between hers. "I've never been so scared in my entire life."

He reached up and cradled her cheek in his palm. "I know the feeling. When you were missing it was like someone plucked my heart from my chest and stomped on it. I should have kept you by my side. I won't make that mistake again."

She frowned, still shaken from the way the events of the day had unfolded. "Isaac and my dad are both in jail. I don't think anyone else has plans to whisk me away to some creepy house in the woods."

"Just to be on the safe side, I'll keep you around so I can make sure of it."

She grinned. "Deal."

"Knock, knock," Dr. Simon said before entering the room. "Good to see you awake. How are you feeling?"

He ran his hand from the side of Laura's face down her arm to settle on top of her knuckles. "As good as can be expected." He shifted to sit up then winced.

She took a step back, but he tugged her toward him.

Dr. Simon chuckled and shook her head. "Seems like Laura might be your best medicine, but we'd like to keep you for a few days to monitor you. Your recovery will take time. You might need help getting around for the first couple of weeks while you fight through physical therapy."

"Don't worry, he won't be able to get rid of me," Laura said, shooting Cade a wink.

"Good. I'm sure he'll listen to you better than the nurses and doctors assigning him exercises."

"Probably."

"I'm right here," Cade said, cutting into the playful banter.

Dr. Simon checked the vitals displayed on the machine beside the bed. "We see that. Okay, everything looks good. For now, just rest. Try to get some sleep tonight, and I'll be back to check on you later."

"Thanks, Doc," Cade said then focused on Laura, tugging harder on her arm until she fit against him on the lumpy mattress.

"What are you doing? I'm going to hurt you."

"You heard the doctor, I need to rest. And no way I can do that without you in my arms. I don't think I can ever sleep alone again."

His words warmed her deep inside and she pressed her lips to his. "Fine. As long as I'm not hurting you, I'll stay just like this until someone kicks me out."

He settled an arm around her and snuggled her close. "I'd like to see them try."

She traced her fingers along his jawline, studying every line of his face. "I love you, Cade. If you would have died without hearing me say those words, I'd never have forgiven myself."

"You don't have to worry about that because I'm not going anywhere. Not now. Not ever."

Sighing, she let her head fall into the crook of his arm and closed her eyes. She could sleep knowing the man of her dreams was finally her reality.

CADE GAVE the room one last look then went in search of Laura. The sizzling sounds and decadent scents of garlic and oregano told him she was in the kitchen frying meatballs to go with the pasta they'd planned for dinner.

He winced, anticipating the heartburn she'd suffer at bedtime.

After Laura had moved in to help him during his recovery, she'd become so ingrained in his everyday life he couldn't stand the thought of her leaving.

So she'd stayed, and it'd been the best three months of his life.

Once he'd gotten almost back to 100%, he'd been able to focus more on her and her pregnancy than himself. Making sure she kept her swollen ankles elevated, rubbing the knots in her back, and running to the store to grab whatever she craved that hour—even if it changed twenty minutes later. His joy came from pampering her and watching her glow as the baby grew inside her.

She'd decided to be surprised by the gender, a decision that excited him as much as drove him crazy. He was a planner, and not knowing made him a little nutty. But he'd do anything for her. For their family.

And now the time had come to make their family more official.

He stopped in the doorway and thanked God one more time for forcing his eyes open to Laura. She stood barefoot in the kitchen, her hair tied on the top of her head and a sleeveless dress showing off her belly. Only a few more weeks before the baby would be nestled in her arms.

A now-familiar tingle of excitement burst inside him. He couldn't wait to meet their baby.

"You've got a second?" he asked, hating to disturb the moment. He could stand and watch her for hours, but there was something more important in the works.

She brushed away a strand of hair with the back of her wrist and stirred the sauce in the pot. "Let me turn the heat down then I'm all yours."

"I'll never get tired of hearing that."

She shot a grin over her shoulder then took the pot off the burner before wiping her hands on a dish towel. "Okay. What is it?"

He held out a palm and waited for her to waddle toward him. He laced their fingers then led her down the hall to the guest room where he'd first held her through the night.

Where he'd first realized he'd fallen in love with her.

"I wanted to show you the crib," he said. "I got it put together and it makes such a big difference in the room. Figured you'd want to see it."

"It's getting so real now."

He chuckled. "Because the basketball in your belly didn't make it real enough?"

She giggled and swatted his shoulder. "You know what I mean. This little one will be here in a couple of weeks."

He led her into the nursery and held his breath. He'd wanted the room to be exactly what she envisioned—something she could take ownership of without compromise. Isaac had taken away some of her excitement over putting the room together. She'd fretted about not wanting the space she created to look anything like what he'd put in that hellhole of a house.

She sucked in a breath and pressed a hand to her mouth. "It's perfect."

"You sure? I can change anything you don't like."

She turned to face him. Tears pooled in her eyes. "Are you kidding me? The yellow walls are so bright and cheerful. The crib is beautiful, and you got the rocking chair from my mom." She traced a finger along the smooth wood at the top of the crib.

"Jude took all the pictures on the walls, and my mom knit the blanket on the back of the chair. But if you don't like it, we don't have to tell her we hid it in the closet."

She picked up the cream-colored blanket and held it to her face. "I love that she's so excited. This is so sweet. But wait... what's that?"

She'd spotted the wildflowers he'd picked and placed on the dresser in the corner.

This was it.

His heart threatened to beat right out of his chest. He sidestepped her and grabbed the flowers before turning to her and dropping to one knee. He folded her hand in his, offering her the bundle of goldenrods and irises with the other. "When we were younger, you'd go into the woods and pick me flowers. I never treasured those gifts—or you—the way you deserved. The last few months you've become the most important person in my life."

Grinning, she took the flowers and held them under her nose. "I was always trying to get your attention."

"Well, you've got it now." He fished the princess cut diamond ring from his pocket. "I never want to take you for granted again. I want to cherish you and love you every day for the rest of my life if you'll let me. I want us to be a family. Laura Metcalf, will you be my wife?"

Her eyes grew wide, and the flowers fell to the floor. "Oh, my God. Are you serious?"

"I've never been more serious in my life. I love you so much, and I love our baby. I want us all together, under one roof, with one last name, forever."

"Yes. Absolutely yes! But I don't think that ring will fit on my sausage fingers." She laughed through her tears as he struggled to put it on her ring finger. "Maybe put it on a chain for now?"

He scooped the flowers off the floor and stood then gathered her in his arms. "You can have whatever you want. For the rest of your life."

He captured her mouth in his then felt a little thump from her stomach. He broke away and chuckled then smoothed a palm over her belly, waiting for another kick. "I think the little one likes our plan."

She grinned and rested a hand over his, giggling when another kick came. "Good, because nothing's changing my mind about marrying you. You're stuck with us."

He pressed a kiss to her forehead and held her close. "Nothing has ever sounded sweeter."

EPILOGUE

Laura struggled to unhook the straps of the car seat as her squealing bundle of joy kicked and squirmed, straining to be free. She couldn't help but laugh. "Isla, you're not helping Mommy as much as you think you are."

Isla clapped her hands and cooed. Her blue eyes were wide, and at four months old, already filled with mischief.

Cade rounded the hood of his truck and edged himself between her and their daughter. "She's excited to take on the world, just like her mother. Let me grab her." He deftly lifted the baby from her seat and held her close, the diaper bag attached to his back. "Daddy's got you now, sweetheart."

Warmth chased away the biting chill from the December air. Her heart threatened to burst with joy. How she'd gotten so lucky, she'd never know, but she'd be eternally grateful.

"Ready?" Cade asked, grinning.

She drew in a shaky breath. "I think so."

The last four months had flown by in a sleep deprived haze. Between marrying the love of her life, adjusting to motherhood, and helping Mrs. Collins get the women's shelter ready, she was amazed she was still standing. If Cade hadn't helped with every single step, Laura had no doubt she'd have suffered from a mental breakdown at some point.

But she'd made it, and now she stared up at the beautiful Victorian house that had stolen her heart months ago. A house that was so much more to her, and hopefully, to so many other women in the area who needed a place to call home. Even if only for a short stay.

Mrs. Collins swung open the screen door and waved her hand over her head. "Come on, you three. Time's a ticking."

Shaking her head, she grinned, grateful Mrs. Collins had healed quickly from her head wound. Not many people her age would be so lucky. Now that the house was ready, she had wanted an official opening for the shelter. A gathering of people who had helped make their dream a reality, as well as investors who were eager to see what their resources had helped create. Hopefully, everyone in attendance would spread the word. Let anyone who needed to hear about Safe Haven Women's Shelter know it was here and ready to help.

She was ready to help.

"Takes us a little longer these days," Laura teased and rubbed the soft, silky blond hair on top of her daughter's head.

Mrs. Collins playfully rolled her eyes then scooped the baby away from Cade. "Sure. Use this little princess as an excuse. Now come on in."

Laura chuckled and glanced at her watch. "What's the rush? We're thirty minutes early."

Cade placed a hand on the small of her back and his touch sent chills coursing down her spine. He kissed just above her ear then whispered, "You'll see."

Her senses were on high alert, but she fought through the sudden jolt of anxiousness and stepped into the foyer.

"Surprise!"

A banner stretched across the ceiling that read *Congratulations* and colorful balloons bobbed along the crowded entryway. Laura covered a gasp with her hand and took in the faces of all the people she loved most in this world. "I...I don't understand. What's going on?"

Mrs. Collins beamed and kissed Isla's chubby cheek. "We're here to celebrate you. This is your dream. You've poured your soul into this old house and created something magical. This town—this community—owes you so much."

Her mom leaned on her cane and slowly walked toward her. Tears shone bright in her eyes. "You're an inspiration to all of us. We're so proud of you, honey."

She squeezed her mom's hand. "I'm proud of you too, Mom."

A light blush stained Nicole's cheeks, and she dropped her gaze to the floor. She didn't like any attention on her and would take no accolades regarding all the work she'd put in to help get the shelter ready, but Laura wanted her to know she saw her. Really saw her. And she understood that each and every step was hard.

Cade hooked an arm around Laura's waist and pulled her close.

She stared into the faces of Matthew and Brandon, Jude and Wade, and all the other amazing citizens of Pine Valley that had banded together to help make Safe Haven Women's Shelter a reality. "None of this would have been possible without all of you. I'm overwhelmed by your support and dedication. You have no idea what this means to me. What this will mean to so many women and children." Emotion clogged her throat, stealing the rest of her words.

Cade pressed a kiss to her temple. "You mean the world to *us*. Your strength and resilience are an inspiration, and I think I speak for everyone when I say we just wanted a chance to play a role in your story."

A smattering of applause and boisterous cheers erupted.

Isla giggled. Drool dripped from her pouty lips.

Joy wrapped itself so tight around Laura she thought she'd burst. She'd worked her fingers to the bone to help build this dream, and now she got to be a part of watching it grow and flourish. She'd get to be there for women who needed someone to give them a hand, a shoulder, or spare room for the night.

She'd give them hope.

And then she'd get to go home to her family—to the little cabin her husband had built and snuggle him and her daughter close.

She hugged Cade, thankful for every blessing in her life. "I love you. Thank you for always believing in me. Thank you for showing me I needed to believe in myself."

Isla lifted her arms toward Laura and kicked her feet.

She took her daughter and inhaled the intoxicating scent of baby shampoo and lotion. Her daughter would always know love—always know security and kindness and compassion.

She'd always have a home filled with family who'd do anything to see her smile.

And nothing in this world could ever be better than that.

SIGN up for my newsletter to read a bonus scene to see how Cade and Laura said their I do's...https://dl.bookfunnel.com/c96orrp2j9

DON'T MISS Marie's story in the second book of Safe Haven Women's Shelter as flees her abusive partner to save her and her baby's lives, propelling her into an unsolved murder case and into the arms of Deputy Owen Wells in Marie's Hidden Refuge.

ACKNOWLEDGMENTS

I'm so excited to release the first book in a brand new series. Safe Haven Women's Harbor is a series centered around single mothers are strong, resilient, and survivers. Laura's Safe Haven was the perfect way to start this series, and I can't wait for the next.

A big thanks to my husband and children. You guys stand by me no matter what, and that means the world to me. Thanks to my awesome critique partners, Samantha Wilde and Julie Anne Lindsey. I couldn't survive a day without your insight and friendship.

Much gratitude to The Editing Soprano for making my words shine, and for the team at Deranged Doctors for designing another beautiful cover.

And mostly, to all my readers. I hope you enjoyed Cade and Laura as much as I did!

Until next time!
Danielle

ABOUT THE AUTHOR

Danielle M Haas is a stay-at-home mom turned author. When she isn't writing fast-paced romantic suspense novels with mysteries to live for and romance to die for, she's busy being a taxi driver to her two busy kids and forcing her introverted self to talk to other soccer moms. Her kids and husband are her world, which is also shared with her hyper Bernie doodle, mini Whoodle, and two sassy cats. Her days are packed with cuddles, kisses, and a brain constantly thinking of new ways to create danger and romance for her next book.

ALSO BY DANIELLE HAAS